M000158300

Death and the Flower

VERTICAL.

Death and the Flower

Six Stories

Koji Suzuki

Translated by
Maya Robinson and Camellia Nieh

Copyright © 2014 Koji Suzuki

All rights reserved.

Published by Vertical, Inc., New York

Originally published in Japan as *Sei to Shi no Gensou*
by Gentosha, Tokyo, 1995.

ISBN 978-1-934287-00-2

Manufactured in the United States of America

First Edition

Vertical, Inc.
451 Park Avenue South, 7th Floor
New York, NY 10016
www.vertical-inc.com

Disposable Diapers and a Race Replica

1

My wife's figure as she tiptoed out of the room stirred the humid early-morning summer air. Despite her efforts not to disturb me, even a slight shift in presence always woke me. Pausing at the threshold, she took form on my retinas as a darker shadow in my dim field of vision.

"Oh," she said, sounding slightly surprised. "I didn't mean to wake you," she apologized, yet didn't meet my eyes, her line of sight wandering in the rear closet instead. What was she staring at with such vacant eyes, thinking what? Most likely she was worried over something stemming from another set of worries, as she was wont to do, rendering herself incapable of action. Anxious that her skirt was too gaudy, for instance, she might be imagining each of her colleagues' gazes until she couldn't get going. It had been that way last morning, too. She'd pull out something from the back of the chest of drawers, stare at it for a while, then put it back. Then take out something else and put it back as well. She appeared ready to skip off work and repeat the ritual all day long had I not told her to knock it off.

"Hey," I called out in a subdued tone, trying to snap her out of whatever meaningless scenario she was ensnared in this time. As if on cue, she pivoted to face me, said "see you later," and made to walk out the front door.

"Hold on a minute." I got out of bed and went after her, stopping her at the foyer. "I go to the daycare today, right?"

She nodded twice.

"I'll have dinner at home, then from seven to nine I've got that private tutoring job," I reminded her. "I'll probably be home by ten, but you don't have to stay up for me."

"Won't he just blow it off again?" Her sly smile was a sign that the chain of worries binding her just a moment ago had evaporated.

"I don't care if he never shows up. I'll still get that tuition money."

I had started tutoring an eighth grader this past April, but as soon as summer vacation came he started blowing off his lessons, never coming home at the appointed hour, probably out goofing around somewhere. Last week and the week before, too, I had waited in his room in vain for two hours.

"Oh, I almost forgot. We're out of disposable diapers. Would you mind getting some?" my wife requested.

We normally used cloth diapers on our ten-month-old daughter, but for bedtime we went for disposable diapers as they had better absorption.

"All right."

"Okay, I'll see you later."

My wife waved exaggeratedly and walked out, her heels echoing loudly in the apartment building's staircase. The sound seemed needlessly, intentionally loud, as if she were feigning high spirits. Like the eyes of a cat, her mood changed rapidly. Just when she seemed to be staring into a black abyss with vacant eyes, she'd burst with innocence. Her rushing down the stairs with her exterior and interior utterly imbalanced always set me on tenterhooks.

My wife had received a diagnosis of neurasthenia six months before we were married. Thankfully, her nerves seemed to have stabilized lately. While she was pregnant, she suffered bouts of insomnia and tinnitus, but perhaps childbirth altered her constitution as she said she slept quite well now. Certainly, her face looked much brighter these days when she went off to work. It seemed we had made the right decision.

With the baby's arrival, one of us had to quit our jobs. We could only leave the baby at daycare from nine to five, after which we would have to hire a nanny for two-fold childcare. The combined cost would easily eat up one of our salaries. Whereas I had switched jobs repeatedly ever since graduating from college, my wife had held a steady job as a school librarian. She didn't much enjoy working with people and I was hesitant to rob her of a workplace she was accustomed to. I was also concerned that her nervous condition might relapse from the strain of raising the child alone. Every single move the baby made would sow seeds of distress, and it was clear she'd worry herself to her wit's end. There was a decidedly high risk of her developing maternity neurosis.

As it happened, around that time the event planning company I worked for was in so much trouble it was on the brink of writing rubber checks, which gave me an incentive to quit. That was in April. Since then, I worked diligently every day, taking care of nearly all childrearing duties while also working part-time as a gym trainer and as a private tutor.

I heard my daughter roll over in her sleep. It was just after seven—two more hours until daycare. Wanting to doze off a bit longer, I burrowed under the covers right next to my daughter, cupped my hands around her head, and drew her closer.

People often say she looks just like me. I myself am surprised by how similar her features are to mine, even in the growth of her eyebrows and peach-fuzz hair. Now our uncannily similar features were laid parallel to each other. While I gazed at her face, I detected the shadow of my father who had passed away the month before. He'd been a textbook tyrant who'd sit cross-legged like a feudal lord and hurl abuse at his wife and children. It felt like an inconsistency that the vestiges of such a man should exist in my sweet little daughter. One was vulgar and forceful, while the other was utterly adorable. And here was I, the intermediary between their blood.

At eight o'clock, I rose and reheated the baby food my wife had prepared. I then woke up my daughter, sat her on my knee, and filled her belly spoonful by spoonful much as a mother bird does for a chick. During the monotonous routine I turned toward the bright sunshine out the window and went over the course of tasks planned for the day.

After dropping my daughter off at daycare at nine, I would return home to do laundry. The cloth diapers had to be washed separately from our underwear and clothing, requiring two loads. Once that was done I had a shift as a trainer at a gym in Meguro until four. In the morning, however, there were very few clients so I would use that time to work out. I really only ended up working with clients for the three afternoon hours. I was single-minded in my training regimen since I'd been admitted to the weight-lifting competition hosted by Kawasaki City. In order to win in the 160-lb class, I assumed I had to lift 1,200 lbs. total across three events: bench press, dead curl press, and squats. Victory was unlikely unless I was able to set a new personal record.

I paused the feeding and rotated my right shoulder. When I kept my elbow pointed towards the ceiling, I felt a slight pain run through my joints. I must have overworked it the day before, rousing an old injury that not even a full night's rest had eased. *Take it easy today*, I admonished myself. I wanted to come in at number one no matter what.

I thought objective recognition of my physical prowess would reaffirm my value for my family.

After the gym shift I would go to the daycare to retrieve my daughter at five. I would pick her up as she crawled to cling to me, strap her into the baby sling on my chest, head home to the apartment, and wait for my wife to return from work. After an early dinner, I would go to Ota Ward for the tutoring session at seven. That bastard Masahiro would probably stand me up again. Since I already knew that was the likely outcome I didn't care to go at all. Time was ripe for a decision: Should I continue working with the Kawaguchi family, or should I find another client? Whatever the case, I had to decide on a stance by the end of the week.

2

The setting sun warmed the back of my jacket as I entered the final approach to Tokyo. The traffic was congested in both directions on Maruko Bridge, which spanned the Tama River, but on a 250-cc motorcycle I had little trouble negotiating the rush-hour roads.

In order to minimize any injuries in case of an accident, even during the summer I always wore gloves, a jacket, and boots. Fitted with duo-toned full fairings stretching from the headlights to either side of the engine and modified into a single seater, my bike was a race replica good enough for the circuit. It wasn't the kind of bike a thirty-something man with a wife and child would normally ride. Back when I'd purchased it, it was the standard for a two-stroke bike. There wasn't a less aggressive model available.

Getting off the bridge and crossing the first intersection I saw a large billboard for a drugstore. Just then, my wife's voice echoed in my mind.

We were out of disposable diapers.

I switched on the directional, pulled over to the left of the street, and parked. I had forgotten all about her request.

The bungee cord that I used to lash luggage to my bike still had to be there in my backpack. I wanted to buy a big economy-sized set, but I wondered if I could even attach the cardboard box to the rear of the bike. From my experience with touring that included overnight stays, I knew that a certain amount of luggage could fit on the bike. It was my vanity that itched slightly. Diaper boxes were always handed over to the customer with nothing more than a proprietary "paid" sticker as they didn't have large enough shopping bags. Illustrations of naked babies tied to the back of an intrepid race replica? At dusk, with the sun still lingering above the horizon, the discordance would surely attract attention.

But you can't raise a child if you're overly concerned with appearances. I got off my bike, took an armful of the discounted diapers stacked high by the entrance, went to the registers at the back, and lashed the diapers to the rear of the bike.

As soon as I walked through the door I was greeted by Mrs. Kawaguchi, who looked to be on the verge of tears. I read from her expression that her son hadn't returned yet for the tutoring session that was supposed to begin. I could sense her helplessness from where I stood, and just witnessing her deep embarrassment was exhausting.

"I'm so sorry, sensei. His older brother's gone to look for him. Won't you please wait inside a while?"

I'd heard the brother was a bit of a troublemaker himself in junior high who'd matured some after getting into a mid-level public high school. Now he was out searching for his kid brother who'd fled the tutor, perhaps having a clue as to where he'd gone.

After being led to the second-floor study I placed my daypack, filled with textbooks and worksheets, at the side of the desk. The desk itself was in disarray. The report card he'd received at the closing ceremony at the end of the semester was still in the same spot it had occupied last week. I indicated the report card with my chin as his mother brought in a cup of coffee.

"I guess that's the reason behind all this." The conspicuously placed report card had been folded repeatedly, a symbol of Masahiro's protest.

"I thought it'd get better…" his mother trailed off ambiguously and looked out the window. Fretfully checking the gate hoping her son was back, she apparently spotted the motorcycle adorned with diapers parked outside. "Oh, sensei, you have a baby?" she asked, her voice suddenly high-pitched.

"Yes. A daughter. She just turned ten months old."

"You're so lucky to have a girl. Boys can be very hard." Her words carried the weight of experience. She was clearly at a total loss about her younger son. That's why I had been summoned.

After quitting my job in April, I'd decided to re-register as a private tutor in Tokyo. I'd taken on such work starting in college, and after graduating I'd done short-term intensive tutoring sessions between jobs as I'd frequently changed occupations. No other job paid better hourly rates while still allowing me to receive unemployment benefits. As soon as I re-registered, I received a call. The client was not looking for a student tutor but an experienced adult, so I was a candidate.

The first time I visited the Kawaguchi residence along with a representative from the agency, Mrs. Kawaguchi showed me a picture drawn on the answer sheet for a final exam. In a box at the top of the page the name "Masahiro Kawaguchi" was scrawled in abysmal handwriting. The rest of the sheet was blank except for an illustration of male genitalia. There was a big "0" above his name in red ink, with two lines under the number. The crude drawing that ran over the tidily arranged answer column for the math problems was childish in the extreme, inferior to specimens found on the walls of public bathrooms. I could see why this drawing was the focus and not the fact that Masahiro earned nothing but zeroes in math and English. At the end of the term, Masahiro's mother had been called in by the principal, who sternly warned that the boy was not likely to be allowed to move on to high school at this rate.

It was easy to imagine how despondent Mrs. Kawaguchi must have felt when the principal and the homeroom teacher showed her that drawing. For a mother of two teenage boys she seemed somewhat weak and unable to properly govern boys. She probably indulged their every whim until they felt nothing but contempt for her.

After seeing the picture, I decided to modify my educational methods. Some male junior high students don't respond until you exhibit brute strength. As soon as I realized Masahiro was one such student, he never stood a chance of taking advantage of me. If he even tried to talk back, I tossed him to the floor and bent back his elbow, holding the lock relentlessly until he apologized. While I resorted to coercion, I also shored up his weak grasp of fundamental course work and praised him lavishly when he arrived at the correct answer. Thus alternating between carrot and whip, I tamed Masahiro to the point where he would complete seven-tenths of the homework I gave him. Teaching isn't that exhausting when there's visible improvement. Seeing students fully respond to all the energy you pour into them is similar to the rewards of raising a child.

As expected, he scored 14 on math and 11 on English on his mid-term exams. The mother was immensely excited when she saw the scores. I lost count how many times she said, "Thank you so very much." I had become a messiah to the Kawaguchis simply by getting the kid's grades up. That day Masahiro and I took a break from studying. We sat in front of the TV and watched a boxing title fight together.

By finals, his scores had improved again. He scored 19 in math and 17 in English. While those could hardly be considered high scores, for a student who'd only received zeroes it was a decent improvement. I had anticipated that his failing grades in both math and English would improve into D's this time around. But the report card he received at the end of the semester still showed a row of F's. He was not rewarded for the first effort he'd ever made towards studying. Yet I was the one who was crestfallen when they showed me the report card.

"Can't be helped, eh, mister?" Masahiro said with a smirk, seeming strangely unaffected, but I couldn't help feeling frustrated. If his grades had risen, our sense of teamwork would be solidified, improving his study habits and thereby easing my task. Four months of violence-steeped investment in his education had been washed down the drain.

The following week, Masahiro didn't come home at seven, the appointed hour. The week after that, he blew me off again. As I had feared, his report card completely destroyed any enthusiasm he'd gained. I wasn't a part of his family; I was simply a tutor hired to work with him once a week from seven to nine, and if the student wasn't home, there was nothing I could do. Ordinarily, you'd expect the father to come tie his son to the desk if need be, but I had yet to see any trace of the man.

As if he'd been waiting for his mother to bob her head and exit the room, Masahiro's brother came to stand at the doorway and looked at me hesitantly.

"Yes?" I said, looking up.

"Can I ask you a question?" He held out a textbook. Apparently he wanted me to teach him in his brother's place.

"Sure," I said, placing the book that I was reading down on the desk and waving him over. I gave him some pointers on how to work a translation. When we paused for a moment, a thought suddenly occurred to me and I asked, "Weren't you out looking for Masahiro?" I didn't know exactly when the brother had returned, but he was back far too soon if he'd indeed gone on a search.

"It's no use. That idiot's with Fujishima," he said bashfully, glancing down.

"Fujishima?"

"Big brother of one of his buddies. He's in a biker gang."

Fujishima. I had heard Masahiro mention the name several times.

He gets pissed real easy. He's mad dangerous, Masahiro had said, his eyes focused on something far away.

"Do you know where he is?"

"Yeah, I think."

"Where?"

"Étranger."

Probably the name of a coffee shop or something that the gang haunted, it was no mystery why Masahiro's brother hadn't tried to bring him back even knowing where he was. The brother was afraid of Fujishima. Seeing them together, he must have slipped back home without so much as calling out to his kid brother.

"Is it nearby?"

"About a ten-minute walk. Go down Nakahara Street toward Tama River and it'll be on your left. It's such a lame old coffee shop you can't miss it."

It would take less than five minutes on my bike. It was almost nine. I had no intention of dragging him back and tutoring him, but I didn't mind checking on him on my way home.

As I was getting ready to leave, the kid smiled broadly with a baby face that resembled his mother's and said under his breath, "You'll be fine, sensei."

"How so?"

"Er, nothing..." he demurred with a vague laugh, but I had a pretty good idea as to his meaning.

You look strong enough. You'll be fine. You'll manage to wrench Masahiro away from Fujishima.

No one had ever told me I was gentle. I was always described as looking tough or intimidating, and I'd been in countless childish fights. I've only had one fight where I put my life on the line, though. Every time I think about it, I can't help but rotate my right shoulder. I can still feel the injuries I sustained that day.

As soon as I graduated from college, I got a job at a small publishing company where I worked in both editorial and sales. One day, apropos of nothing, I started thinking about the dream I'd had when I was a boy of becoming a ship's captain. It grew inexorably until I could no longer tolerate living on land. Day after day, visions of the ocean washed against my brain with the ebb and flow of the tides and refused to fade. I was sure that if I neglected the urge it would haunt me for the rest of my life. I worked up the guts to quit my job and used connections to gain passage on a tuna fishing boat whose home port was Muroto Bay. At that point I had already proposed to my wife, so I asked her to wait for just one year. I figured after a satisfying year on the seas I'd never dream about becoming a sailor again. My purpose was not to fulfill my dream but to be freed from it. But my wife-to-be, as she was left behind, interpreted my sudden behavior in two ways and spent the year in a state of worry faced with a pair of alternatives. Should she trust my word and wait for a year, or had I in fact just politely dumped her? She must have tried to recall my speech and conduct countless times to guess my true intentions. The more she thought about it, however, the more violently she swung between both extremes, and her panic eventually wrecked her nerves. I was entirely responsible. That's why when my wife got pregnant and grew hypersensitive, hinting at a possible relapse, I had no choice but to devote myself completely to her and our baby, at least for a little while.

Just four months into the sea journey that caused my wife's neurasthenia, I got into a fight that nearly cost me my life. Things like reason and logic have no place on a tuna fishing boat. As a first-timer there were many things I didn't know, and the fishermen merely blamed me for my ignorance. If I screwed up even a small part of the operational protocol, a fist accompanied by a shout flew straight for me. The sullen whirlpool created by men cut off from the rest of the world was something utterly unique. After working day after day under the watchful eye of the Grim Reaper, it was understandable that they'd lose their temper over small issues. But one day I jumped clear over the line.

If a shark was caught, it was the newbie's job to gut it. Naturally it fell to me to do the dissection, as it was called. I thought I was working efficiently, but I heard someone holler, "Hurry up, asshole!" I jerked up in time to see a foot-long buoy flying towards me. I ducked at the last second and turned around to see the buoy tumble across the deck. People often use the term "snap." When that buoy rolled and bounced off the gunwale, I actually heard an internal fuse blow in my neural circuitry. If that buoy had hit me right in the head it could have been fatal. At this rate, I constantly risked getting murdered. I had to break out of the situation ... and chose my target. The boatswain that threw the buoy was solidly built, could easily lift a 200-lb tuna, and was rumored the strongest man on the boat. Roaring like a beast, I charged him.

He looked stunned for a moment by my sudden defiance but soon threw down his tools and rose to the challenge with an "All right!" Other men halted their work and thronged around us. We grappled and punched each other for several minutes under their watchful eyes. I was engrossed. I remember how I felt a strong urge to kill him. If the chief fisherman hadn't been there, I imagine we'd have fought until one of us was dead. When he waded in to part us, I couldn't even stand up. My right collarbone was damaged, my left middle finger was broken, and I'd lost three upper front teeth. The boatswain hadn't fared much better in the physical damage department. Yet my recompense was substantial. After that brawl, the fishermen's attitudes toward me did an about-face. None of them tried to pick on me again. In fact, they were much more respectful towards me, and my life on the boat improved dramatically. *Why hadn't I tried that earlier?* The memory still fills me with regret.

Perhaps smelling that savage blood, most people I meet for the first time are intimidated by me. I've been vaguely aware of this for some time. Even so, Masahiro's brother's words made me see myself in third person.

A little after nine, I stood in the foyer and asked Mrs. Kawaguchi, "What should we do next week?" I knew already that I'd be blown off again even if I showed up on time, and I was starting to get fed up over being paid fifty thousand yen per month when I wasn't teaching. I didn't mind quitting right then. My income would take a temporary hit, but I'd find another student soon enough. I couldn't get involved in another family's troubles.

"Please come again next week. I will do whatever it takes to have him here."

Her pleading eyes clung to me. I was her last ray of hope. The golf bag—a totemic substitute for the man of the house—placed next to the shoe rack just inside the front door intimated this mother's powerlessness. I felt some compassion for this family with the absentee father.

"Let's see what happens for just another week," I said, promising to return, and took my leave.

3

I stood in front of a pane of smoked glass on which the word "Étranger" was painted and peered inside the well-lit interior of the coffee shop, but there was no trace of the boys. When I moved to the side, I triggered the automatic door, and smoky air billowed out and assaulted my nostrils. I could sense frustration and youthful irritability in that smoke, which probably hadn't been inhaled. The place could seat maybe a dozen people but was devoid of customers. Fujishima, Masahiro, and company seemed to have gone elsewhere, leaving just their smoke behind. A sense of relief came over me. I got on my bike and headed home to where my wife and child waited.

I was speeding along Nakahara Street towards the Tama River. Just as I passed Ring Road No. 8 I noticed headlights moving oddly in my rear-view mirror. A car, behind me at an angle, was tailing me closely. The road was pretty empty, so the way the car was maintaining its distance was unnatural. It could only be following me. It was a gunmetal gray old-model Celica with a dropped suspension.

I slowed to allow it to pass me, but the Celica slowed down as well to maintain the distance. I could see the metalwork of the Maruko Bridge over Tama River looming before me. The two lanes per direction shrank to one on the bridge. In order to go straight onto it, I had to merge right. The Tama's water level was low, and in the damp, humid summer night, I could see on its surface the lights of the residences in Shin-Maruko where my wife and baby waited. I might still make it back in time to bathe my daughter.

As soon as I had that thought, I felt wind pressure from the side. The Celica that had been tailing me had sped up and was now next to me on my right. I turned to face forward again. The metal guardrail of Maruko Bridge was fast approaching. I quickly downshifted twice and sped up to try and pass the Celica and get into the right lane. The engine revved with a high-pitched noise and my body jerked backwards from the sudden acceleration. An ordinary car couldn't possibly match the two-stroke race replica's acceleration rate. But this Celica's engine was apparently modified, and the car stayed right next to me the whole time not falling behind an inch. The distinct sound of the enhanced engine echoed eerily.

For a split second, I couldn't make a decision. Blocked as I was by the Celica, I couldn't switch to the right lane, and if I continued on, I would strike the guardrail of the bridge. Was that what they wanted? There was no time to hesitate. I slammed on my brakes. I knew as soon as the dropped Celica blocked my route that it'd be dangerous to get into some kind of match. But apparently blocking me from merging wasn't all; the Celica swerved towards me from the right after I hit the brakes.

"The hell are you doing?!" I yelled from inside my helmet.

A mere bump from the Celica's passenger side door to the bike's right handle made me lose balance. Realizing I couldn't avoid a fall, I purposely pulled the bike down and tumbled rear-first onto the pavement. The lights flickering in the distance disappeared for a second, and I felt a wash of nostalgia for the touch of my daughter's milky-scented skin. Death was very much on my mind. As my back and knees struck the asphalt, I rolled several times, and I could see my bike sliding across the street, spraying sparks. The friction from the asphalt drew a trail of them in the humid summer air and the gas tank seemed ready to ignite at any moment. More than the sounds or anything else, that vivid image etched itself into my mind. The tip of the clutch lever broke off and the abrasion from the pavement sharpened it into a blade. The bike slammed into the guardrail tire-first and rebounded with great momentum, right towards me. They say if you fall off your bike at thirty miles per hour you end up rolling for several dozen yards. Of course you wouldn't be able to change direction while you rolled. I mentally braced myself. The remnants of the bike would crash into me, ensnare me, the honed clutch lever would pierce my body...

Just then, I felt like I was being hugged by something smooth and resilient. I had no idea what was happening.

I thought maybe I'd heard a rubber band snap as well. The next instant, my field of vision was swallowed up, and in the darkness I went still.

I must have passed out for just a few seconds. The cold feel of the pavement on my cheek gradually revived me. My hearing returned at the same time and I could hear a tire spinning idly right beside my ear. The faint sound of the river flowing past seemed to rise skyward only to come down like rain. Lying prone on my back, I slowly raised my head to check my abdomen. I tried moving my limbs. When I tried too hard, pain coursed through me. In the distance I saw the dark Celica that almost killed me stopped near the bridge entrance. A rear passenger window opened and a small youth leaned out to check the damage. I could tell it was Masahiro without even bothering to squint. The Celica abruptly took off in the direction of Kawasaki.

A passing car stopped and its driver leaned his head out the window. "Are you okay? Need an ambulance?"

I stood up and hopped lightly from foot to foot to double-check for any injuries. Still wearing my helmet, I shook my head and tried to call back, "I'm fine," but found I had no voice. The driver gave me a dubious look, gently honked his horn once, and sped away.

I noticed that disposable diapers were scattered all over the road. A sound like a rubber band snapping, the soft, pliant sensation... Here lay their source. Before the bike collided with me, the bungee cord I'd used to lash my freight had snapped, tossing the diapers between the motorcycle and myself. As though to prove this, the clutch lever had skewered a number of torn plastic bags containing several diapers each.

I started gathering the scattered diapers and returning them to their plastic bags. I knew they were beyond usable at this point but didn't want to leave them like litter on the street.

I righted the bike, pushed it across, and leaned it against the guardrail. The left side that had scraped along the pavement had suffered the most damage, the fairing warped beyond recognition. The tailpipes were ruined, and looking head-on I could see the front suspension was twisted. I couldn't tell if it was oil or gasoline, but a black, glossy liquid from the bike dotted the pavement like so much blood. As time ticked by, I grew increasingly agitated. I found myself imagining that the liquid splattering the asphalt was not oil but my own blood.

I headed home, pulling the badly mangled bike over Maruko Bridge. It wasn't an easy task to haul a bike with a twisted suspension on badly bruised legs. In order to get it to move straight forward, I had to force down the handles as if I were laying her down. Just ten yards was an arduous journey. I was drenched in sweat from head to toe before I'd even crossed the bridge.

I parked the bike on the side of the road some distance away from my apartment and walked the rest of the way home. I stopped for a minute at the outside stairwell of the apartment building, held my breath, and listened. Somewhere in the sultry, windless August night I thought I heard a baby crying. When I held still and strained my ears but heard nothing more, I decided it was just my imagination and felt a wave of relief. It seemed I had made it back in time for night feeding. It was just past eleven. My wife and baby were probably in a heap, asleep.

Ours was an old two-story apartment building with identical two-room floor plans and four apartments per floor. We just barely afforded it with our combined incomes. Even if you tried to ascend quietly, the rusty metal staircase swayed and creaked. The right-hand corner apartment on the first floor was the only one that still had lights on, the TV set faintly audible. Everybody else seemed to be asleep. There were no lights from our next-door neighbor with the rarely seen husband, but I could hear the sound of water trickling. Household wastewater seeped like so many dregs from the shabby apartment where a tired mother and her children lived a very cramped lifestyle.

The kitchen was immediately by the foyer, and in the back were two tatami-mat rooms, one 75 square feet, the other about 100 square feet.

The tiny light was on in the smaller of the two rooms that functioned as our bedroom, and a hint of the steam from my wife and daughter's bath still hovered in the air. My discomfiture gradually ballooned in the lingering humidity. I flung off my jacket and t-shirt and pulled off my jeans, which had torn at the knees, and threw them at the floor. I sat cross-legged on my discarded jeans and checked myself over for injuries. I noticed blood trickling from below my knee. Looking at the wound carefully under the light, I could see that several small specks of rock had eaten into my skin. Using a pair of tweezers I tore open the skin to dig out the specks and disinfected the wounds with hydrogen peroxide. Aside from that, my left elbow was bruised and oozing blood. There was no damage to the elbow section of the jacket; only my skin had torn. Considering the condition of the bike, it was almost unbelievable that I'd walked away with such light injuries.

If the diapers hadn't been there to cushion me from the impact, things would doubtlessly have turned out much differently.

As I wiped the sweat from my body with a cold towel I measured out a cup of water and brought it to a boil. I added the proper quantity of powered milk to a bottle then poured in the boiled water. After the powder completely dissolved, I put the bottle inside a basin filled with cold water to cool it down to an appropriate temperature. I wiped off the wet bottle with a cloth and checked that it was just above body temperature by wrapping both hands around it and holding it against my cheek. I'd made my baby cry several times because the milk was too hot, but now I was so used to the process that I no longer had to drop the milk on my tongue to make sure it was right.

Leaving the sliding screen between the rooms open, I sat on the threshold and drew the baby to me. I took the utmost caution to avoid making any noise and put my daughter, breathing peacefully in her sleep, on my lap. I gently touched the nipple on the bottle to her tiny lips. Instinctively, she latched on with her eyes still closed. I could see the milk in the bottle decreasing rapidly from her powerful suction. It was as if vitality itself were passing from my hands to my daughter and accumulating in the depths of her body. Under the weak fluorescent light I stared at the dwindling milk. When my wife was diagnosed with mastitis and could no longer produce any milk, she was pitifully depressed, but if it hadn't been for that, nursing my daughter would have remained a job well out of my reach.

When the bottle was empty, I lay down in the narrow space between my wife and daughter and stared at the dark ceiling for a while. I was still agitated and didn't get the sense I'd fall asleep anytime soon. I turned to my side and looked at my daughter's sleeping face. Perhaps sensing my presence, she stretched out her tiny hand to touch my cheek. Her hand wandered across my face until she found my left earlobe, which she grabbed and squeezed tight. As she did so, her expression relaxed, and her breathing resumed the rhythm of deep sleep. Unable to roll over with her hand clutching my earlobe, I felt tears well up in my eyes like it was the most natural thing. Thanks to her touch I got a powerful sense of my own value and presence. That tiny hand had very nearly lost what it relied on. My body trembled.

The one thing I could do for my family was put myself on the line for them. Yet, a capricious show of spite had nearly snuffed out my life. Imagining my family's future without me pained my heart. The scene of the accident came flooding back. I had never before felt such appreciation for my own life, nor had I ever been as mindful of death. At the same time, I felt sharp anger roiling up for the would-be murderer at that Celica's wheel. I didn't know who it was, but I knew Masahiro had been in the backseat. Why block me from switching lanes and run me off the road? Was it just some game?

My daughter stretched out her other hand, stuck it between my head and my pillow, and grabbed my right ear. With both of my earlobes squeezed and my face pinioned in place, I cursed at the dark figure of the driver and clenched my fists tight.

Perhaps sensing my tension, my daughter's hands squeezed my earlobes even harder. She must have been dreaming about food. She made munching movements with her mouth and drool dripped down her face. I relaxed my fists, wiped off the drool with my finger, and touched it to my tongue. It had a slightly milky flavor.

4

The next day, after a light workout at the gym, I took the afternoon off to visit the Kawaguchi residence. I made the unannounced visit in the hopes that I might catch Masahiro at home since it was summer vacation, but unfortunately he wasn't there.

"Oh my, did he have a lesson scheduled today?" Mrs. Kawaguchi inquired, perplexed.

"If you don't mind I'll wait until he comes back," I announced and stepped inside. I hid my shoes behind the golf bag in the entryway so I'd remain undetected. "When Masahiro gets home, please don't tell him that I'm here, no matter what," I cautioned his mother.

Moved by such a display of responsibility from a private tutor, Mrs. Kawaguchi meekly thanked me, bobbed her head repeatedly, and withdrew.

I waited for about an hour in the air-conditioned room. While I sat at the desk, it struck me how my efforts over the last four months seemed to have been a total waste. I'd come to believe in Masahiro once his grades had shown some improvement. Yet now the distinctive cruelty of youth spooked me. I had no desire for any further involvement with him no matter how much money they offered me.

It wasn't hard to understand why Masahiro had gotten zeroes on his exams. Who wants to admit to having inferior abilities? Choosing to run away before discovering one's limits—of course that was tempting. The first escape was drawing a penis across the answer sheet. The drawing loudly exclaimed: "I'm too special to do stupid things like take tests." But as he started to study in earnest, he began to see it himself. Strive as he might with a private tutor, he lacked the ability to turn his F's into D's, even. So he plotted another escape, this time by blowing off his tutor. How could he be saved? How could I teach Masahiro that we each need to muddle through whatever predicament we're in with whatever abilities we've been blessed with? I was chagrinned, but what really pissed me off was that Masahiro's avenue of escape had nearly cost me my life.

The front door slammed shut and sprightly footsteps echoed up the staircase. Fed up with waiting, I swiveled the chair around to face the door. When Masahiro opened it and took one step inside, he froze in place.

"Hey. Long time no see," I said calmly and raised a hand in greeting.

Masahiro, eyes blown wide, muttered, "Sensei…"

He turned on his heel and tried to run away. I caught up with him at the top of the stairs and kicked him in the back. Masahiro lost his balance, tumbled down the stairs, and struck his head on the landing wall. He yelped a needlessly dramatic "Ou-u-ch!"

Just as his alarmed mother set foot on the stairs, I grabbed him by the collar and hoisted him up. "It's nothing," I reassured Mrs. Kawaguchi, whose eyes looked ready to pop out of her head, and dragged Masahiro back up the stairs. Along the way, in a fit of rage, I slammed his face onto the edge of a stair. His bottom lip split open, caught between his teeth and the rubber edge on the wood, and blood dribbled from his mouth. Masahiro merely moaned rather than attempt another exaggerated reaction.

Once back in the room, I threw him on the bed and closed the door. He was trembling from fear. Perhaps judging that no excuse would work, he kept his mouth shut.

I put a pencil in his trembling hand and placed a notepad in front of him. "Write down the name and address of whoever was driving the Celica last night."

From the subdued way I'd spoken, Masahiro seemed to sense that I meant business. He obediently wrote "Fujishima" on the notepad in phonetic script and cast down his eyes. "I don't know his address," he mumbled. Ordinarily he would have said, *How the hell should I know?* Today he was minding his manners.

"You don't know where he lives?"

Rather than reply, he started drawing a map. He was still terrible at drawing. He marked an X behind a Mitsubishi Motors located just before the gas-pipe bridge over the Tama River. I studied the map and mentally reconfirmed the local geography.

"Shimo-Maruko is the nearest station, right?"

Nodding, Masahiro licked at the blood on his lips and shed tears. Shoving his weeping face into the mattress and standing up, I made to leave the room.

Masahiro's sobs grew louder as though he was begging me not to leave. "Diapers..." he seemed to say.

I stopped mid-step, turned around, and gave voice to a question that suddenly came into my mind. "Why did you do it?"

"Sensei, those diapers…" he trailed off.

Was it possible Masahiro and his buddies had messed with me without knowing who I was? It wasn't impossible. Riding a race replica motorcycle with an economy-sized box of diapers strapped to the back would certainly have drawn attention. A biker gang running along Nakahara Street might have found it amusing to harass such a rider. Perhaps at first Masahiro had no idea that it was me. He did realize when Fujishima sideswiped me but didn't dare rein in the guy, only leaning out the rear window to check if I was alive. Come to think of it, maybe I'd seen a somewhat worried look on his face in the dark last night.

A favorable interpretation, while possible, didn't kill my anger. After all I'd almost died.

"See ya."

I closed the door just as Masahiro tried to say more.

Before I ever found Fujishima's house, I discovered the black Celica. It was parked, its left tires perilously close to a drainage ditch, on an empty road dividing a residential area from an industrial zone. With my back flush against a factory wall so as not to fall into the ditch, I went around to the passenger's side. There was a two-inch long scratch on the back of the side mirror. It had to be from making contact with my bike's right handle the night before. I thought it had been the door, but apparently not. The bike had lost balance when the handle caught on the back of the side mirror. As I stared, uncontrollable anger tore through me. It was completely unfair that while my bike was mangled beyond recognition, only a tiny scratch marked the car that had done it. Safe inside a metal box, not even showing his face, the guy had casually placed a total stranger in mortal danger.

I grabbed the mirror with both hands, twisted it up hard, and wrenched it off the car. I tossed it into the ditch. Still not sated, I punched the center of the door. The wall at my back prevented me from really winding up but I managed to make a dent right under the window. That still wasn't enough to ease my wrath. In fact, it was like pouring oil onto fire. I kicked at the dent with my knee and made it larger. I glanced over to the driver's side and saw that the key was still in the ignition. If the driver hadn't simply forgotten, it meant he was planning on coming right back. Wising up to the futility of mauling an inanimate foe, I slipped out of the narrow space and leaned against the wall to wait for the driver.

The deserted street behind the factory led straight to the bank of the Tama River. Having found the car, I didn't feel like looking for Fujishima's house. Even if I did locate it, I couldn't simply walk in. So just what was I trying to do now? Would I call out to Fujishima and scold him for his dangerous stunt? I closed my eyes. When I showed up uninvited at Masahiro's place and asked him for the driver's address, I wasn't thinking about what I was going to do once I found the guy.

I saw the image of my wife and daughter waiting at home for me to return. I was beginning to regret coming all the way out here lured by my anger. If I came face to face with Fujishima, there was no telling what I would do. Even if he were pure scum, I'd be forcing my family into dire straits. How was I supposed to relieve myself of this rage anyway?

I made to walk away as though suddenly unbound. Just then I heard footsteps trotting along the black asphalt.

A skinny male who looked to be around twenty was coming toward me out of the darkness. The guy seemed to have come out from the house just three doors down. He whistled as he trotted pigeon-toed and with a slight hunch, both hands in his pocket, toward the Celica. Convinced that he was Fujishima, I found myself working the stiffness out of both of my wrists. I relaxed my shoulders, held my elbows in place, and bent back my wrists, stretching them up and down.

I pushed off the wall and started walking. Fujishima was reaching out for the door handle, but surprised to see me appear from the car's shadow, he froze and stopped whistling.

Right now I'm motivated not by logic, but instinct. So I'll have my body decide. Will hatred for someone who almost robbed me of my life win, or will I let it pass to safeguard me and my own's peace?

The decision would be made the second I passed Fujishima. If he angled for a fight, I wouldn't hold back anything. Since there was hardly any foot traffic past the banks of the Tama River, we wouldn't draw any attention. We could brawl as long as we wanted. Not merely breaking a couple bones, I might kill him, if necessary, to end the scourge that was him. The same hands that washed a baby's cloth diaper would take a man's life. As soon as I had that thought, the scene in the alley framed by the gray wall stood out with clear contours. Pounding along to the certain rhythm of my pulse, a sense of being alive once again gushed up in me. My field of vision seemed to narrow as well, with Fujishima as its focus.

The guy seemed the type to throw a fist before opening his mouth if he was given a dirty look. Yet, instead of planting his feet, he swallowed whatever he was about to say and drew back his shoulders. He stared at me speechless. Whether or not he'd sensed my murderous intent and panicked, his cheeks went slack and his eyes unsurely evaded mine.

The servile smile that crept onto his face was hard to miss. It was a fawning, ugly smile. I felt a wash of disgust. He was nothing more than lowlife, hardly worth laying a finger on. The truth was that he was not capable of anything. As soon as his face went slack, the fighting instinct that had swelled to bursting within me vanished. I would gain nothing from taking him on.

As he passed by, I brushed shoulders with him on purpose. Having tried to sway away, Fujishima lost balance and put one hand on the Celica's roof. I glared at him with every ounce of scorn I could muster, then briskly walked off.

By the time I turned the corner on the alley, I had regained a measure of calm. The blood that had pooled at my temples melted back into my body, and the scenery dissolved into typical blandness. In that easeful moment I casually considered fathering another child. Walking north along the Tama River's bank, I mumbled to myself: *Another girl'd be fine by me.*

Irregular Breathing

Any outside air was completely shut out by the thick glass of the windows of the ICU. Even so, when I woke up in the middle of the night I sensed, though I couldn't actually hear, rain falling.

I rose from the guest cot and gently lifted up the curtain. Cupping my left hand to my brow to block out the light escaping from the nurse station, I wiped the moisture off a fogged-up window. As my eyes adjusted to the darkness, the U-shaped inner courtyard gradually came into focus. The branch of a cherry tree in the courtyard reached all the way to the intensive care unit on the third floor, close enough to touch were I to reach out. The leaves weren't wet.

Unconvinced that my intuition had been incorrect, I tried looking up at the sky. Thanks to the interference of the balcony upstairs, only a slender band was visible. It must have been cloudy since I didn't see twinkling stars in the rectangle. When I shifted my focus downwards, I could see raindrops dripping off the leaves of the cherry tree. The three main branches drooping in different directions rustled in the rain, leaves and boughs swaying every which way, perhaps due to a breeze. I felt a strange satisfaction at predicting rain just as it started falling.

As I stood gazing, the chill from the March night began to seep into my body. When I moved away from the window, the white lines of the hospital bed where my wife lay seemed to float outside, the reflection transposed over the image of the cherry tree.

The ICU had two parallel beds. The other one had become vacant only early yesterday morning. In the gloom, the pure white of the freshly washed and starched sheets stood out symbolizing the "death" of the human being who'd passed away in the room.

My wife and I were the only ones on this side of the glass partition with the nurse station. The sound of breathing filled the room. Not my wife's, but the respirator's. Some sort of piston was compressing and delivering air, and a mechanical sound that was neither a hiss nor a wheeze recurred at a consistent interval. This noise was why my sleep was shallow and I often woke in the middle of the night while keeping my wife company. There was nothing in the natural world that sounded similar. The closest comparison was Darth Vader's respiration from *Star Wars*.

I checked the level of the IV and the readings for the various monitoring devices stored in the column-type unit. There didn't seem to be anything amiss. The machines were running smoothly, just as they'd been before I'd fallen asleep. The nurse had only asked me to keep a close eye on the level of the IV, but I couldn't help eying all the readouts on the monitors. I didn't have an accurate grasp of what the numbers signified. I just checked to see if they were still the same.

I walked around to the foot of the bed and looked down at my wife's face. The respirator's tube stretched from her mouth down into her throat and was affixed to the entrance of her trachea with a balloon-shaped section. A feeding tube was inserted from her right shoulder, and the tube that drained away urine hung down under the bed. There were two systems of gentle, artificial currents flowing through my wife's body. Aside from those that sent in nutrients and carried out excretions, there was another tube stuck in her bandaged head that flushed out the blood pooled inside her brain. The tip of this tube passed through a small hole in the temporal region of her skull and nearly reached her cerebral cortex.

Peering closely, I could see pink fluid running through the thin, transparent tube. They were dissolving the blood that had built up between the pia mater and the arachnoid membrane in order to flush it out of the body. If the hematoma resulting from the bleeding was left untreated, she could become hydrocephalic, the attending physician had explained.

Finding myself curious once again about the exterior, I opened the curtains and gazed into the courtyard. At some point it had started raining in earnest and the white hospital walls as well as the cherry blossoms and branches were getting a thorough soaking. The blossoms in particular looked as though they would fall off at any second, yet they held fast to the tips of the branches. Wet, the flowers' hues looked more vibrant.

My wife had suddenly taken ill the afternoon before

last, but it felt like a great deal of time had passed since then. The night before, I'd sat in the hospital's waiting room without even dozing off until the operation ended. A single day's events felt like they spanned several days.

After a checkup at the gynecologist, my wife had taken a bus ride home then collapsed. She'd crumpled onto the sidewalk while stepping off the ramp. It gave me the chills to wonder what might have happened had she collapsed just a little bit later. The bus stop was right in front of our apartment. If she'd lost consciousness at home, alone since her husband was away on a business trip, she'd have stayed that way overnight and been too far gone. Her operation had been urgent. By the time I'd rushed over to the hospital in a panic after receiving a call from my sister-in-law summoning me back, the surgery had already begun.

Subarachnoid hemorrhage.

Being told what she had didn't make it any more sensible for me. My wife was only thirty years old. Thinking her too young to suffer a stroke, I only felt irrational anger brewing in me. In the waiting room my sister-in-law relayed the surgeon's explanation to me. My wife's vascular media was inherently weak and she'd had a cerebral aneurism. Walking around pregnant had made it rupture.

Said some people are more prone to it than others. How awful. If it's hereditary, will I get it too? my sister-in-law muttered, her brows furrowed, quite personally worried as she shared her summary.

The nine-hour-long surgery was a success. They applied specialized clamps to the ruptured vessel and to the bases of two more aneurisms that were about to burst, then closed up her skull. There were no notable effects on the infant, and indications were good for the mother. Yet it was too early to relax. Developing cerebrovascular spasms a week or two after the onset of internal hemorrhaging was a possibility, and if that happened, she'd be beyond help. Apparently, there was no established treatment for cerebrovascular spasms.

For two nights in a row now, I was only sleeping in fits and starts. I was tired, but my nerves were too tense to allow me to fall into a deep slumber.

I sat on the edge of the metal bed frame and gazed at my wife's body for a while. I gently laid my hand on the swell of her belly, noticeable even under the blanket. I felt a kick. The seven-month-old fetus had struck the walls of its mother's womb with its limbs. It was our first baby, conceived in our fourth year of marriage. We already knew the gender. About a month ago, we'd watched as the fetus appeared on the ultrasound monitor at the gynecologist's. We simultaneously cried out "Ah!" at the sight of a protrusion between the legs.

"A boy?" asked my wife.

The doctor merely laughed and didn't respond, but his smile said as much. Without a doubt, the baby was a boy.

Placing my hand under the blanket to feel more of the unborn child's presence, I froze. I sensed that something was out of joint. The atmosphere of the room was mainly dictated by the sounds of the respirator. I couldn't help but think that its rhythm sounded slightly off. The pause between the loud inhalations and exhalations that engulfed the room seemed longer than usual. The lengthy break was making me fear that the breathing cycle had ceased altogether. As I listened intently, a few sudden breaths that sounded different from before broke the silence. Then it was all quiet again.

Shocked, I stood up and checked the orange numerals floating on the monitor of the respirator, but there appeared to be no irregularity. The reading was still the same. I listened closely and waited for the rhythm to resume. *Hnff, hnff.* With what sounded like a pair of choked coughs, the respirator started to wheeze. As if it had just finished a burst of intense exercise or was suffering an asthma attack, the apparatus had completely abandoned the cyclicality that characterized machinery. It almost sounded like a ferocious beast was breathing through a megaphone.

I thought maybe my wife's and the respirator's breathing rhythms had gone out of sync to cause this trouble. Perhaps the function that automatically adjusted the pace was glitching. Since the machine was my wife's lifeline, the slightest anomaly set my nerves on edge. I put my ear close to her chest, checking for irregularities in her breathing. Her chest rose and fell slowly, almost without a sound. Her face showed no signs of suffering. Her plump cheeks occasionally creasing as if she were smiling, her expression was the picture of serenity.

There was a nurse call button in the unit that would send one running over as soon as it was pressed. The station on the other side of the glass partition was brightly lit, and three young women on the night shift were chattering with lively, glowing faces. I wondered what they were talking about. Seated around a table, they periodically bended at the waist in fits of irrepressible laughter. Were I to open the door, the clamor and scent of young women would tumble into my world where the respirator's sound was everything. A single pane of glass severed the two worlds and their polar opposite lights and sounds. Neighbors to death, these women who nevertheless scattered carefree smiles shone and exuded youth.

Instead of pushing the call button, I knocked on the partition with the back of my hand twice. There was no reaction. Too engrossed in conversation, they couldn't hear me. I knocked again. Rather than the sound, the sight of me rapping on the glass caught the attention of one of the nurses. She gently touched the shoulder of a chubby colleague who had her back towards the partition. Looking around, the alerted nurse immediately stood up and walked over to the door and turned the knob.

"Is something the matter?" she asked, poking only her head into the ICU and standing on her toes. The vestiges of lighthearted conversation still lingered on her face, her heart still in that bright world.

"There seems to be something wrong with the respirator," I complained, indicating the unit with my chin. The nurse peered into the dark world and strained to listen for a while from where she stood. Then she walked into the ICU, closed the door, and hurried over to the front of the machine.

She stared at the monitor in silence. Tilting her head in thought, mumbling a few words under her breath, she bent over to check the unit's back and confirmed that all the cords were connected. Yet, the respirator's constricted breathing continued to wash over the room. The nurse looked up at the ceiling then moved her gaze to the wall. Her stout figure stood on tiptoe as if she were trying to catch distant echoes. The room still sputtered violent coughs, but her mind seemed to be wandering somewhere far away.

Striding back to the monitor, she stood facing it. Then, for some reason, she slapped the cuboid top section, the main body of the artificial respirator, with the palm of her hand. And slapped it again. A chill ran down my spine. It felt like she was slapping my wife's chest. The artificial respirator had stepped in for my wife's lungs and was a part of her now. I'd lost track of where the machine ended and where her internal organs began. Yet, as if to prove that continuum, the machine gradually started to regain its regular rhythm. The monitor even looked up with hang-dog eyes.

"How do you feel now?" the nurse asked the machine. She gave a satisfied nod and started making her way back to the bright place where her colleagues waited—with hurried steps, assiduously avoiding eye contact with me, acting as though nothing had happened. The door closed and the room was as it was before.

I was not convinced. A medical device, supposed to represent the height of precision, getting its act together thanks to a spanking? This wasn't some TV set with bad reception. Any irregularity directly impinged on my wife's life. *Still*, I told myself, *they may be young, but the nurses are the pros here.* A pro had determined that nothing was amiss so maybe I just needed to relax. The machine was fully back in rhythm and indeed sending a sufficient amount of air to my wife's lungs. To begin with, the whole time the unit was on the fritz, she hadn't betrayed any sign of suffering. The irregularities in the machine hadn't affected my wife in any way.

I glared at the respirator's monitor for close to ten minutes. The breathing was regular, maintaining fixed intervals. All clear, it seemed. I thought I'd get some shut-eye and lied down on my cot.

Before I knew it, my breathing had synched with the respirator. My body must have aligned with the vibrations in the room. Once in sync, it was impossible to break away from that rhythmic spell, just like it was difficult to walk against the beat of a loud marching song. It actually felt comfortable, being one with the room. I was reminded of my wife in Lamaze class learning how to breathe during delivery. She'd been quite humorous conveying to me how all these pregnant women on their backs all moved their stomachs in and out as the midwife called, "Now breathe in, now breathe out…"

It was ridiculous. We looked like beached seals.

The image of her smile as she demonstrated floated into my mind.

I had multiple dreams in succession. It seemed my sleep was still shallow because as soon as the machine's breathing reached my ears, the dreams would shift course, bubbling up and fading away with no connecting threads. Reverie and lucidity pushed and pulled like waves.

I awoke for good in the middle of a dream. Vexed over being unable to send any air into my lungs no matter how hard I sucked, I woke up clawing at my chest. For a minute or so, I must actually not have been breathing. In fact, the moment I sprang up, I inhaled a mighty gulp, relishing the taste of air. I tried to remember the dream I'd been having. Maybe I'd been drowning. Yet I couldn't recall there being any water. Rather, the blue of a clear sky above some highlands clung to the folds of my mind. When I pressed my palm to my chest, I could feel my heart pounding as if I'd swum the full length of a 25-meter pool without surfacing.

My eyes went straight to the clock. It was a little before three in the morning. My mind was in a fog, and I kept trying to get it into gear. Something was strange. Something was missing. A sound that was supposed to be there...

My spine froze.

The respirator's stopped!

Kicking off the blanket, I jumped out of bed, knelt by my wife, and placed an ear to her chest. Her steady pulse and gentle breathing reached my ears. I nearly collapsed from relief. I turned around and checked the monitor of the respirator to find that the orange number was unchanged. Numerically, at least, it seemed to be working fine. Only the sound had stopped.

Still crouched, I reached out a hand toward the main body of the respirator. It was cold to the touch. I tapped it on the side. Then I slapped it a few times with an open palm, watching my wife's expression as I did so. I'd have to stop the second it started to affect her. When I dealt a fifth blow, strongish, the machine's breathing suddenly revived. Just as I had upon waking from my dream, the respirator took a few wheezing, devouring breaths. It fell silent again then emitted a moan-like cry. Without thinking, I took my hand off the machine. It seemed to me as though the solid black body had trembled from the intermittent breathing. When I touched it again, the same spot held a bit of warmth. Although I understood that my own body heat had simply transferred to it, the warmth was redolent of the raw presence unique to creatures. The respirator was alive. As proof, it was spewing phlegmatic noises now. My father who'd passed away a year ago had often made such a phlegmy, gurgling sound right before he died. I'd never mistake that peculiar cadence.

Was my wife's life force getting sucked out by inorganic machinery? Her breathing was as steady as a machine, while the machine's exhibited an animal irregularity. I tapped its side a few times with my right hand to calm it down and looked around the room. I was trying to think if a replacement respirator could be set up quickly should the unthinkable happen. There was another column-type unit the same height in the corner of the room, but it was covered with a sheet, perhaps because it hadn't been used in a while. That meant the person who'd died in this room the morning before had been on the same respirator that was now in use. A number of doubts flickered rapidly through my mind. Had this respirator been beset with the same symptoms, choking, unable to breathe, while that patient was on it? Had its irregular breathing killed the patient?

An emotion closer to anger than fear welled up in me. Were the nurses intentionally ignoring the machine's poor condition? They'd have nothing to gain by losing a patient.

Without hesitation, I pressed the call button. As soon as the same chubby nurse from before rushed into the room, I was on my feet.

"What the heck is going on with this thing?"

I was trying to hold back but ended up practically hollering. The nurse stopped still, gathered her hands in front of her chest, and closed her eyes.

"Please do something. It's clearly malfunctioning," I pressed.

With a look of sorrow on her face, the nurse knelt in front of the respirator and hit the side of the machine with a loose fist. I was about to ask how long she was planning to stick to such a slapdash method, but then noticed that tears were running down her cheeks.

"Please have a cup of tea with us in the next room," she

offered, sniffling.

I couldn't leave my wife alone in a room where a full-blown machine rebellion seemed imminent.

"Please don't worry. It happens all the time."

While I hesitated, she stood up and started walking towards the door. There was nothing I could do but to trail after her in silence.

I followed her into the nurse station and closed the door behind me. With the machine's moaning perfectly shut out, an altogether distinct world emerged. Partitioned by a simple plate of frosted glass were two realms whose sounds, colors, odors, and even room temperature completely differed, antipodal neighbors across a mere thin membrane.

Still standing, I cupped the proffered tea in both hands and sipped at it a few times. If the nurse had something to say, I wanted to get it over with. Preoccupied with the world next door, my eyes kept glancing beyond the partition.

"It was lung cancer," the nurse began abruptly.

I could only look at her, stupefied. That use of the passive voice. "Who are we talking about?"

"Mr. Tadashi Niimura."

I had never heard the name before, but I instantly made the connection. "The patient who passed away yesterday morning?"

"Yes."

After that, as if to clear my suspicions one by one, the nurse who had struck the respirator kept on talking. What the irregular breathing that filled the next room signified... What internal organs and each and every cell in them desired... If I weren't hearing it right there, this was hardly credible talk. Oddly, though, I wasn't scared. Perhaps any explanation allayed fears better than just letting suspicions fester.

When the nurse was done speaking, she put her soft palm over the back of my hand and whispered, "Don't worry, the machine is working fine. It's just the sound."

Her cherubic face looked grown-up for that brief moment. Maybe it was her constantly working under the shadow of death, but her expressions and tone were persuasive beyond her years. That must have been why a preposterous story had come across as realistic.

I put my empty teacup on the table. "Thank you for the tea."

The nurse simply gave a childlike smile in reply.

I sat for a long while on the cot, resting my chin on my hands. Occasionally I remembered to stretch forward and tap on the chest of the respirator. Every time I did so, the irregular breathing settled and the sounds receded. The echoes would soon fade away as well.

Tadashi Niimura, 47 years old. He was the one who had died 24 hours ago in this room. His left lung had been riddled with cancer, and he'd undergone a pneumonectomy of his entire left lung last September. He was making good progress for a while, but at the start of the new year his coughing and phlegm production took a turn for the worse. Exams revealed that the area from the carina to the right bronchial tube was getting clogged up by cancer. It was inoperable, so all they could do was make it easier for him to breathe.

It wasn't hard to imagine the suffering of the patient. His left lung was already gone, and when he tried to breathe in with his remaining one, the airway was mostly blocked.

Beyond the intricate branches of the bronchial tube his alveoli awaited in vain. The exchange of gasses between the arteries and veins must also have been stymied. I could almost hear the cells that made up the lung screaming for oxygen. In terrible agony, he'd indicated numerous times, *Hit my chest. As hard as you can!* When a nurse did as he requested, peace would return to his face just for a moment. Tadashi Niimura had spent three weeks in such a state, in this room, before finally expiring 24 hours ago. The entire time, the respirator had operated continuously as a substitute for his lungs. Why would there not be any residual echoes in the machine? I was leaning towards buying it. The room had an air that made you buy it.

Dawn was about to break. In the end I'd barely slept a wink. The belabored breathing was now so subdued that I had to listen for it. Wholly unaffected by all the groaning, my wife had slept on with a peaceful countenance, her breathing steady, and I was impressed by her strength. On the one hand were cells that had perished screeching with pain. On the other hand was my wife, within whom cells repeatedly multiplied in the others' wake, sleeping indifferently through a nightmare of a night as if it had all been someone else's problem. Cradling, in her belly, cells that were fated to perish too someday, she submerged them in amniotic fluid, provided them with nutrients, presided over their growth. The bodies of a fetus and its mother were connected by various tubes. Just like an ICU.

I opened the curtains to see heavy clouds moving across the rectangular strip of sky. The rain seemed to have stopped sometime ago, and the cherry leaves were drying off.

The door opened forcefully, and a nurse came in with

a fresh IV bag. I had completely forgotten that it was nearly time to change it. The level on the hanging IV fluid was just about to dip below the final mark. The nurse changed out the bag with practiced hands, checked the monitors, and looked into my wife's face. Perhaps it was in response to the nurse's shadow—my wife's eyelids slowly started to open.

Key West

The islands stretched right in the middle of the straits in a column from the southern tip of the Florida peninsula. Steel bands of highway straddled the gaps like rainbows, leaping at each island just as a flat stone might across the surface. The car rose and fell in gentle arcs, sometimes nearly level with the sea and looming far above it the next moment. They'd reveled in this scenery yesterday evening as well before a night in Key West at the very tip of the archipelago. Today they were headed back. They'd return the car to the Miami rental service in the evening, retrieve the missing suitcase at the bus terminal, and then depart for their final destination, New York.

Tatsuro Atsumi slowed down, reluctant to surrender the pleasurable sensation of flying at low altitude over the ocean's surface. Just then, he noticed a small island on his left and recalled its dark silhouette against the sunset as they'd driven past last night. Now it was afternoon, and in the bright sunlight the island was a tangle of lush greenery peeking out of the sea. It had a very different aspect at midday than at twilight, but there was no doubt it was the same island. Yesterday, they'd stopped the car to gaze at it, entranced. Now, once again, Tatsuro felt himself strongly drawn to the island and decelerated. As he plumbed his heart for the source of the connection he felt, it dawned on him. Four years ago, he had painted a portrait of his late wife. The island he'd placed in the marine background looked a lot like the one he was passing by at that very moment. One was an imaginary island in a dreamy oil painting, and the other an actual island. Yet, their colors, sizes, and even distance from the shore were strikingly similar. Tatsuro had seen the island for the first time on this round trip, but it was as if a figment of his imagination had sprung forth from inside him and come to life.

Without bothering to signal, he pulled the Ford rental over and appraised the island with a mind to getting there. It was small, probably a little over a mile in circumference. A dilapidated gray pier was visible on the facing side—but no buildings, let alone any sign that the island might be inhabited. *A deserted island...* The words held a nostalgic ring. The place was within reach, so close, right before his eyes. It lay about a hundred yards off, only a few minutes' swim. For a 43 year old, Tatsuro was lean and mean and a confident swimmer thanks to his strict weekly regimen at the gym pool.

"Might be worth it..." Tatsuro murmured to nobody in particular.

The remark wasn't directed at his daughter, Yuko, who sat in the passenger seat beside him; he was simply confirming his intentions by stating them aloud. Yuko, having just turned twelve, wasn't strong enough to swim that far.

She was introverted and not very athletic, much preferring drawing over exercising—a trait possibly inherited from Tatsuro, who was a high school art teacher.

"Huh?" Yuko said, then fell silent, her face fearful. She offered no further reply. Especially after their misfortune six years ago, she had an aversion to being left alone.

"I'll only be twenty, maybe thirty minutes, so could you wait here?" Tatsuro insisted.

"Hurry back," Yuko replied curtly without even seeking an explanation for the sudden swim. "Don't go too far," she added.

Tatsuro stood on the shore and looked at the color of the sea he was about to cross. Perhaps due to the ebbing tide, most of it had the hues of the shoals, the sand and undulating seaweed visible under the surface. About midway across was a long, ellipsoid sandbar that ran parallel to the shore. Only in the short stretches between the shore and the sandbar and the sandbar and the island, darker green waters suggestive of depth swirled. He wouldn't be swimming across so much as wading. Tatsuro told his daughter this to see if she might be willing to come with him after all. She shook her head and said, "Just hurry back."

Tatsuro stripped down to his underpants and waded out into the water.

What had made him want to set out for the piddling island? Sure enough, there was a stretch of water deeper than his height between the shore and the sandbar, and after swimming across the swift current and standing in knee-deep water on the sandbar, Tatsuro had fresh doubts about his whim. Time and again, senseless impulses beset him. Moving to New York with no particular plan in mind a year after finishing art school. Responding to an opening for an art teacher at a private high school upon his return. He'd acted on a whim both times. After the school had implemented a five-day week, he sometimes took his wife and children for aimless drives on Friday nights. That night six years ago was one such occasion. He'd forced his wife and children, who weren't in the mood, to come along, to satisfy his whim, and driven westward on the Tomei Expressway. It wasn't raining, but the road started getting wet near Gotenba. Just a while earlier, a sudden downpour had passed through. Oncoming trucks sent up sprays of water across the windshield so Tatsuro turned on his wipers now and then. Thanks to droplets of water dancing in the darkness like a mist, however, visibility was remarkably poor. Their three-year-old boy tried to move from the back seat to his mother, who was riding shotgun, and got wedged in between the front seats. Tatsuro glanced at his son, distracted, and shifted his gaze back to the road to see two red brake lights growing rapidly closer. Blurred by droplets of water and bloated to gigantic proportions, the redness pressed upon his brain as a hideous form. Even now, Tatsuro could remember that color. Whenever that red light, scattering as if through a prism, appeared in his dreams, he stiffened his right leg.

A little calmness could have subjugated his panic. Foolishly, he slammed on the brakes. The wet road, the hard braking, hydroplaning... The car stopped responding to the steering wheel, collided into the median barrier, then spun further. Screaming and a roar like earth tremors mingled and swirled inside the car. Eventually a darkness like black painted on black filled the interior and all sound faded into the distance, the tremors slipping away as well. How long he was unconscious Tatsuro couldn't well fathom. As soon as he came to, he recovered his hearing and felt pain in his forehead. Tensing all of his limbs to straighten himself out of an unnaturally twisted position, he struggled to comprehend the disaster that had befallen him. The center pillars were bent, the front windshield was shattered to bits, and the crumpled hood of the car obscured most of his vision. He heard moaning from the back seat, but only one voice, and his wife was not in the seat next to him. The impact had launched her through the windshield and out onto the street. Imploringly, Tatsuro extended his line of sight out onto the lanes and strained his eyes. Right in the middle of the road, about thirty feet away, he discerned darker patches lying next to each other. Thrown from the car, Tatsuro's wife and son had been run over by one truck after another and plastered into the road as dark stains on the asphalt.

Halfway across the sandbar, Tatsuro turned and glanced back towards the shore. The highway ran level just three feet above the sea, and the red Ford sedan sat in a parking area framed by subtropical foliage. The driver's side door still hung open. Tatsuro couldn't hear it from where he was, but the local FM radio channel must have been playing over the sound system. Between a stand of mangroves and a rocky area in front of the car Yuko scampered after marine life. Her bright orange t-shirt was easy to spot even from where Tatsuro stood. She sat down on a rock and kicked with both feet to disturb the clear water's surface, then stood up and crab-walked along the beach. In the background, a truck streaked past.

About a hundred feet from the island Tatsuro halted and looked back toward Yuko again. She was sitting on the rock now, her feet dangling in the water this time. Maybe she was tracking the progress of some gaudy-colored molluscan denizen of the subtropics.

Maybe I should turn back, a voice of warning echoed somewhere in Tatsuro's mind. He was beginning to understand why he was feeling so uneasy. Bottomless dark intimations rose up strand by strand from the tips of his feet and amassed in his very core, freezing him.

Like a child stuck in a tree, unable to climb up or down, Tatsuro found himself paralyzed on the sandbar. The island was right there; it'd be quicker to go on than to head back. He wanted to be free of the creepiness brushing at his toes as soon as possible. When he'd begun to swim, and when he'd first dipped his feet into the sandbar, he hadn't imagined this rapidly mounting dread. That initial step, the sand had felt surprisingly soft, enveloping his foot up to his ankle, but he'd relished the underground coolness against his toenails. In the blaze of the subtropical sun the shallow water was warm, and the mixture of sand and mud was the perfect texture to soothe his flushed feet. By the time he had taken a few dozen steps, however, the coldness underground seemed to clutch at his legs; when he'd waded more than halfway, it turned into a chill up his spine. An instinctive sense of danger flashed vague images in the back of Tatsuro's mind. After a few more steps, the images sharpened into a specific notion, and pellucid words etched themselves into his bosom:

Watch out. Something lives under the sand you tread!

Tatsuro stopped in his tracks and once again considered heading back to the shore. Yet he already knew, without even turning around, that he was much closer to the island. The only immediate way to deal with his dread was to set aside all thoughts of returning and to complete his passage to the island. Once he set foot on dry land, he might shake off his fear without ado.

Tatsuro began to wade towards to the island again. He took long strides, minimizing contact with the sandbar as much as possible.

Why did I decide to cross over to the island?

The same question repeated over and over in Tatsuro's mind as he probed his memory. Then, he recalled an image from two nights earlier.

A bus terminal against the backdrop of a city at night was diametrically opposed in mood to a subtropical string of islands dotting the Florida Straits during the afternoon. Yet, from the perspective of Yuko waiting back on the shore, there were definite similarities between Tatsuro and the suitcase that had disappeared into the darkness of the bus terminal two days ago at midnight. Both receded steadily away into another realm. The suitcase, swallowed up into the darkness and lost, echoed Tatsuro's present state.

The night after they had left New Orleans, their bus had made a short meal stop of about an hour in Jacksonville. Nearly all of the passengers had disembarked to eat at the café in the terminal, returning to the bus only when it was almost time to leave. When about half of the seats were filled, Yuko grew agitated, glancing nervously at her father. Just as the bus was readying to pull out, she leaned over her father's lap, peering out into the darkness beyond the window.

"Hey, our suitcase, it's going...that way," Yuko stated in little bursts. She squinted, anxiety clouding her features. Tatsuro looked outside, following her gaze. Just below the window, the bus driver was handling the customers' luggage.

Death and the Flower

Three duffel bags sat in a row on the pavement next to him. As it was a terminal stop, he was sorting out the bags of passengers who were transferring. But Yuko's gaze was focused on something farther away. There were city lights in the distance, and between the lamps of the terminal and the darkness beyond wriggled a lump of some sort. Its form was indefinite so Tatsuro couldn't be entirely sure of what he saw then. A rectangular, suitcase-sized mass appeared to be pulling away at a leisurely pace all by itself. Appeared to be... Nothing more. Depending on how you looked at it, it was just a dark stain on the concrete. Every vein in Tatsuro's body throbbed. He averted his gaze before the memories could come rushing back.

Though he sensed what she sensed, Tatsuro ignored his daughter's warning. Even looking in the direction she pointed was repulsive. He had to tell himself that it was some bad joke. For a while thereafter, Yuko continued to whisper that their suitcase was creeping about the parking lot of its own accord instead of sitting in the cargo hold under their seats, but Tatsuro shut her out feigning sleep. Even after they had become a family of two, Tatsuro and Yuko had traveled overseas together sharing a single suitcase. As a teacher, Tatsuro had long summer vacations, and their trips had become a tradition. This year, the plan had been to traverse the U.S. via intercity buses, from Los Angeles to New York, over a period of two weeks. The suitcase contained their clothing and other travel essentials. According to Yuko, it was strolling away into the night...

Having sorted the luggage, the driver returned to his seat at the front. He had already confirmed the number of passengers, so they were ready to depart.

66

Slowly, the bus began to move. Her hand on her father's knee, Yuko pressed her face against the window and stared out into the darkness. As the bus turned, the centripetal force pushed Yuko and Tatsuro back against their seats, and when they could lean forward again, the bus was already headed down the highway in the opposite direction from the darkness into which the suitcase had receded.

Upon their arrival at the depot in Miami yesterday morning, Tatsuro turned in his claim tag to retrieve their luggage. The attendant ran this way and that but in the end failed to find their suitcase. Sure enough, it was lost. A staffer from the bus company explained that the suitcase must have been loaded onto another bus by mistake, apologized repeatedly, and guaranteed to recover the suitcase, which must have been ferried to the wrong terminal, by the following night. Unwilling to waste a day waiting for the suitcase's return, Tatsuro and Yuko picked up a rental car as planned, departing for Key West with only the carry-on bag containing their valuables.

When he was almost at the end of the sandbar, Tatsuro felt pain at the tip of his left foot. It didn't hurt badly, but he was worried over the cause. It had felt like stepping on a pointy pebble, but there could be none floating amidst soft sand, and if there were one it ought to have sunk rather than impart any pain. Spooked, Tatsuro jerked his foot up out of the water, lost his balance, toppled forward, and hit the sea's surface. A whack sounded deep in his ears. Something felt strange. The pier, which had caught his eyes just as he fell, loomed larger and larger in his consciousness.

Parts of the wooden pier were rotten, and Tatsuro had to

tread carefully to avoid falling into the sea. He sat down cross-legged on the pier and inspected the spot where he'd felt the pain. There were two red dots at the base of his big toe on his left foot. They oozed blood when he squeezed the flesh around them. Something had stuck him. Tatsuro tried to recall sea creatures with spikes. It didn't hurt badly so he decided he was fine and rose to his feet.

The periphery of the island was blanketed in a sad excuse of a beach, and old fishing gear littered the area near the pier. Amongst them were white styrofoam spheres the size of basketballs that, upon closer inspection, revealed little navel-like knobs run through with a thin, vinyl rope. Lower on the beach a lattice shape sprawled buried in the sand. It was an old fishing net, exposed to the elements, tattered and torn. The styrofoam balls must have served as floats to keep the net near the surface, but Tatsuro couldn't quite visualize the trapping method. The island must have served as a fishing base some ten or twenty years ago then fallen into disuse before being abandoned completely. Here and there a few globes of pale green glass sat peeking out of the sand. Some were broken, and Tatsuro would have to watch his step when he walked on the beach.

He turned and looked back towards the highway. A thumb-sized Yuko was waving at him. It felt strange to be in an objective position vis-à-vis the highway. It was as if he'd become a point on the canvas gazing back at himself as he painted. Every so often, the sound of a passing truck would arise from another dimension and fade away. Tatsuro waved back at his daughter, finished crossing the pier, and stepped onto the beach. He thought he could hear his daughter's voice calling to him from behind.

The noises that issued forth from the jungle felt familiar to Tatsuro. They reminded him of the first train of the morning and its echoes that flowed into his apartment in Tokyo. He was on the third floor so he couldn't see the carriages directly. When he awoke early, he often listened to the rhythmic sound interrupting the predawn stillness like the rush of a faraway breeze accompanied by a metallic clankity-clank.

Guided by the noise, Tatsuro moved this way and that as he approached the trees and caught sight of an animal trail that led into the island's interior. The narrow passage wasn't immediately obvious; it was lined on both sides with rows of palm trees and apparently long covered in grass and low brush. The intermittent rumblings from deeper within were like a welcoming voice greeting a visitor. Tatsuro stood at the head of the trail and peered inside. The vegetation was dense, casting overlapping layers of shadow on the sand to form a starkly dappled pattern of dark and light. In particular, the rays that filtered through the thickest growth cast white mottles on the sand as on a cut of prime beef, and come to think of it, his wife had been fond of dresses with such patterns, while she was still among the living... Gazing on, Tatsuro's thoughts wandered in unexpected directions. He felt a strong urge to explore deeper.

He glanced back over his shoulder and glimpsed his daughter out of the corner of his eye. She was trying desperately to get his attention. She waved her arms and seemed to be calling to "Papa," but Tatsuro couldn't hear her voice. Leaving it be, he started walking towards the interior.

The sand beneath his feet was hot in the sunny spots, but in the shade it was cold enough to make him catch his breath. Gooseflesh rose on his arms and back, but it was oddly comfortable and he didn't want to turn back. He was lured by a premonition of rare vistas. A world full of unusual displays of color might unfold before his eyes and provide inspiration for the oil painting he was working on.

The temperature in this climate in late August was ferocious, easily over 100 degrees. Although it was fairly dry unlike the humid heat he'd experienced in New Orleans, merely retreating into the shade did nothing. Tatsuro dripped with sweat and his throat was parched.

As he walked further, the narrow trail became more of a path, and he saw clear proof everywhere that a number of people had walked through here long ago: scars from knife slashes in the trunk of a palm tree, eight metal pipes hanging from a branch. The rusted pipes appeared to be a sort of wind chime that played cooling sounds when a breeze blew, but at present the air was completely still, and the pipes showed no sign of moving, let alone making music. Farther ahead, a plastic basin lay at the base of a tree, and beyond it a wooden stool, half-buried in sand. Evidence of prior human habitation was becoming more and more salient. Then Tatsuro spotted what looked like the roof of a house poking out of the dense foliage. Soon he saw several roofs. As he continued to walk, he came to a clearing bordered by a number of abandoned buildings—a former village.

All of the buildings were made of wood. Traces of brightly colored paint still clung to their walls in places, but for the most part it had peeled away exposing the bare wood underneath. About half the wallboards were still intact while the other half had rotted away. A few of the houses were roofless, and the roof of one had collapsed and crushed a rotting wall.

Tatsuro counted the buildings. A total of fourteen single-story buildings, all the same size, stood in rows of seven each on either side of a long, rectangular clearing. At the end of the open space was a larger two-story building, clearly different from the homes, behind which hid a pitch-black shadow of an object. It lurked, motionless, holding its breath, only its dark silhouette sticking out at the sides.

Tatsuro halted when he saw it. While the thing was mostly hidden by the building, from its contours he had a fairly good idea what it was. Still, he couldn't bring himself to believe it. As he walked down the center of the clearing, he found himself visualizing nocturnal Tokyo. The cars streaming by on the Metropolitan Expressway, the creak of steel against steel as a train rushed by—such were the keynotes of the city at night. Back when Tatsuro's family was still intact, he'd go to bed in his room, the children's clamor replaced by an enveloping silence, and hear an urban symphony seeping in from outside. He'd often lulled himself to sleep imagining, one by one, the sources of those sounds.

When Tatsuro rounded the building's corner, he beheld the very thing he had imagined. It wouldn't have been at all out of place in the city, but in the middle of a tiny island, it was incongruous enough to be nauseating. It was a passenger car from a train, the kind once pulled by a steam locomotive.

The bizarre juxtaposition made Tatsuro shudder. He felt as if he'd wandered into the depths of a labyrinth. He shot a nervous glance back towards the path he'd taken. It was still there—he hadn't stumbled into another dimension. If he retraced his steps back to the pier, he'd be able to see the highway with cars traveling across it, and in the foreground, his daughter, Yuko, waving to him. Faced with utter inexplicability, everything started to seem uncertain. At the same time, he was curious and wanted to make sense of his discovery. Approaching the black iron passenger car, Tatsuro looked it over. Standing on his toes to peer through the window, he saw rows of double seats divided by a central aisle. It was a very old-fashioned rail car, the kind you might see in a Western, and only the window frames were made of wood. There was no locomotive; somehow, only this passenger car had been left here. The hook-shaped coupler was badly corroded and looked as if it might crumble away at the slightest touch. As Tatsuro reached out, he felt something metal and hard in an unanticipated direction—at the soles of his feet. He cleared the sand away from where he was standing. A rusted rail emerged right underneath. When he continued to brush away the sand, Tatsuro unearthed a train track running across the center of the island, perpendicular to the path leading back to the dock. The tracks would lead to the shore at either end, that much was clear even without further investigation. Twin rails that came from the sea, crossed the island, and disappeared back into the sea… A rail line that ran parallel to the highway. Tatsuro felt the strength drain from his body, and he sank to the ground.

After a few moments, however, he came up with an interpretation. One day two decades ago, when he'd been playing artist in SoHo after finishing his studies and moving to New York, Tatsuro had been in bad need of pictures of subtropical scenery for a piece he was painting. He'd obtained a book of photographs of Key West that included the following description beneath an aerial photograph of the highway that linked the islands:

"Until forty years ago, it was a railway, not a highway, that extended from the southern tip of Florida through the Florida Keys. But one night a ferocious hurricane tore the railway to pieces, and the current highway was built in its place..."

It was only now that Tatsuro recalled those few sentences.

Right. In the past there really was a railroad here.

Once this realization occurred to him, the unlikely discovery of tracks on a deserted island ceased to shock him. Until sixty years ago, a rail line had traversed this island rather than where the highway was today. The derelict pier that hinted at a former fishing hub, the two-story building that resembled a station, and the remains of a settlement surrounding the clearing... In light of all of these traces, it made better sense to think that the railway used to run here across this island.

Tatsuro's sense of dread abated. Now that there was a plausible explanation, the veil of mystery was peeled away. The atmosphere seemed to take on a different cast, and even the sounds were assuming a more mundane aspect.

His spirits restored, Tatsuro strolled through the clearing, stopping in front of each abandoned edifice to peek inside. He pictured the people who had resided here more than sixty years ago. How had they lived? It was easy to imagine that fishing had been central to their livelihoods. When the weather was good, they would head out in their fishing boats, and on stormy days they would remain indoors. Even if there were long spells when the haul was poor, the island was rife with nature's bounty. Vegetable protein grew high overhead throughout the year in the form of coconuts and breadfruit. They weren't quite isolated from civilization. The train that linked the island to the peninsula could bring in various goods as necessary.

The image taking shape in the back of Tatsuro's mind was that of a utopia in which families lived carefree, easy lives. But one night, a ferocious hurricane had ravaged the entire region, tearing the village and railway to shreds. The highway built to replace the railroad had bypassed the island, and the community had died off and fallen into extinction.

Just like my family, Tatsuro muttered, and once again he was filled with turmoil. He felt out of joint, as though his senses had somehow become divorced from his body. All of a sudden he was struck by the odd notion that the settlement before him was an artifice of his mind.

His wife had liked to tell him, *There's a lot of hidden meaning in scenery, sometimes what you're thinking is projected whole onto what we see.*

She had been a devoted follower of a certain new religious sect and given to issuing such strange pronouncements. At times she told simple fortunes.

Someday for sure your paintings will come into demand.

She'd said that, too, and just as she'd predicted, lately Tatsuro's art was experiencing a surge of positive appraisals. In a year or two he'd be able to quit his teaching job. It was ironic that his wife, who had wanted more than anything to see him succeed as an artist, hadn't lived to see it happen. She'd never learn that two years or so after their family was sundered, Tatsuro—who'd failed to muster much creative drive while steeped in the warmth of his family—would come by a preternatural level of focus, the quality of his art progressing by leaps and bounds as a result. What he expressed on the canvas was precisely his emotional devastation, but people found his use of colors remarkable: *a precarious fragility, as it were.* For Tatsuro, painting was the act of plastering over the two voids that had formed inside him. He simply hadn't been able to go on living without his art. He could hardly survive if he left the two dark stains unattended.

The wooden wall he was facing was painted yellow, and just in front of it, a pipe jutted up from the ground. It looked like a snake rearing up to strike. The neck of the thin black pipe stretched two feet high straight up from the ground and ended in a spigot that hung down. No wonder the Japanese word for spigot was "snake mouth."

I wonder if it still works?

Naturally Tatsuro had no intention of drinking the water even if the mouth spouted any, but he tried anyway. It was badly rusted and refused to turn at first, but after several tries it finally yielded, spinning freely and rising in his hand. Tatsuro took a couple of steps back and steadily observed the spigot.

For several moments nothing happened. But just as he began to walk away, he heard a faint groaning noise from somewhere. The vague commotion drew closer, resembling the mingled voices of a large crowd rather than the sound of plumbing. When the noise reached the spigot, the upright pipe began to shake, waving its neck back and forth like a living snake, and spewed muddy water from its mouth. As the flow continued the water gradually grew clear, but even then the pipe continued to rock, blasting the ground with bursts of water that seeped instantly into the earth. What sort of plumbing ran beneath this island? Where did the water come from? Somehow it made Tatsuro think of the veins and blood running through his own body. Then, once again, he remembered something his wife had said.

The earth itself is a living organism.

A gentle breeze carried a blend of voices and a mechanical sound to Tatsuro's ears. He turned around. Voices of several people. A boat's motor. It was coming from the direction of the pier. Quickly, Tatsuro headed back the way he came.

Hiding in the brush, he espied the pier and spotted a fishing boat approaching the island. A shirtless man stood on deck, still holding in his hand the t-shirt he'd just removed. His hair was almost completely white while his skin was darkly tanned. On the bridge, a much younger man steered the boat. The shirtless man stood at the prow and shouted loudly at the man on the bridge.

Tatsuro strained his eyes and ears. He could hear the shirtless man's voice clearly, but the words were completely unintelligible. It wasn't English, nor Spanish, another language common in these parts. It was a tongue Tatsuro had never heard before. But from the man's body language, Tatsuro understood that he was directing the young man on the bridge to approach the pier. The shirtless man readied a mooring line.

Once the prow of the boat was lashed to the pier, two boys came barreling out of the cabin. They ran around the deck carrying thin rods that looked like fishing spears, and the shirtless man was shouting at them to stop: *It's dangerous.* Even though Tatsuro didn't speak their language, he somehow understood what they were saying. Just then, someone else who had been crouched on the deck rose up. It was a middle-aged woman who wore her hair pulled back in a ponytail. The woman appeared to be tending to fishing gear. She spread open a net and began to fold it.

The shirtless man stepped down onto the pier and walked

towards the boat's stern. The woman tossed him a mooring line, and the man fastened it to a cleat. Now the boat was secure. The motor had fallen silent, and in the brief moment of quiet the passengers stepped onto the pier. The young man and the shirtless man transferred the day's catch from boat to pier by hand. The children shouted and ran straight towards the grove where Tasturo was hiding, but the adults called them back and made them help out. All of their faces were alive and exuberant. The feeling they radiated was that of returning home after a day's work.

We're home!

Just watching them filled Tatsuro with relief too.

The heaving ruins behind him began to take on a warmer hue at the same time. The village, abandoned until now, was coming back to life and breathing, ready to welcome people home.

It didn't take Tatsuro long to realize that what he'd taken for a deserted settlement was in fact still inhabited. The artifacts of everyday life he'd missed just peering in from the threshold slumbered in the interior. He was confident that if he returned to the village now, he would detect the sure scent of human life.

So it hadn't fallen into ruin after all.

Even with the railroad destroyed, one family had chosen not to leave the island, and their descendants remained here to this day. Indeed, the plumbing still worked. Perhaps there was even electricity.

Hadn't fallen into ruin.

Tatsuro murmured those same words over and over again. In his excitement he held his breath, half rising from his crouch as he continued to watch the five islanders who appeared to be a family. Then it dawned on him how things might seem from their perspective.

What do I look like to them? The answer was simple. *Nothing but an intruder.*

Had he shown his face and greeted them before they'd docked, perhaps he could have alleviated any suspicions. But now it was too late. If the children discovered a stranger in the bushes, they would probably scream. In response, the white-haired man would come running to investigate, and Tatsuro would be unable to explain himself. Even if he managed to convey through gestures that he had parked his car by the side of the highway and swum across to the island, if they asked for a reason, he would have no answer. After all, he himself didn't know why. Why had he swum across to such an island? First and foremost, Tatsuro doubted that they could communicate by speech. The white-haired man was aged but muscular and fit. The younger man who had been steering on the bridge had a friendly face, but there was no telling how vicious he might turn.

It seemed that the safest option was to leave the island before they noticed him. Before the five of them came up this path with their fishing gear, he'd cut sideways through the brush and get to the beach and then hit the surf. Loath to set foot on the sandbar again, Tatsuro intended to circumvent the elliptical shoal altogether and to swim all the way. The strait was only about a hundred yards across, but the detour would make his journey much longer. Still, it was far preferable to wading across that cold, slimy sandbar.

Tatsuro was walking north, parallel to the highway, through low plants that dotted the subtropical waters. He couldn't see the pier from where he was, so naturally the islanders wouldn't be able to see him, either. When the water was above waist-deep he began to swim—quietly, using the breaststroke, to disturb the water's surface as little as possible. Glancing towards the highway, he saw that Yuko was walking along the shoulder, parallel to him, matching his pace. She waved vigorously and jumped repeatedly, and it was clear that she was calling out to him at the top of her lungs. Yet he couldn't hear her. Treading water, he craned his head and strained his ears, but not a word reached him. Mostly he just wished his daughter would pipe down. Here he'd given the islanders the slip and if she didn't stop shouting they might notice. Though unlikely to do him harm, there was no need to aggravate them.

Tatsuro treaded higher and used the momentum to dive beneath the surface. He swam underwater for a few strokes, came up for air, and went back down, scanning the bottom to locate the sandbar. Near its edge where it sloped down into deeper water, he caught sight of two rope-like shadows tangling and swaying back and forth. At first he took them for seaweed, but soon their movements indicated that they were animals. They had streamlined heads at the end of their thin, speckled bodies.

Sea snakes.

There were crater-like depressions all over the seabed. From each hole a snake protruded, its tail hidden in the sand. Not just their heads but the better part of their slinky bodies undulated in the water. Tatsuro stopped moving and let his limbs go limp, allowing his body to float up. He timorously glanced towards the sandbar where the water was barely two feet deep. There, too, was a similar spectacle—countless long black cords wavering and craning towards the surface.

Some poked only their heads out of the craters, while others extended almost their entire bodies, their heads nearly reaching the water's surface. The entire sandbar was a nest of sea snakes.

Tatsuro finally understood why, wading across it to reach the island, he had felt such creeping unease and dread. The skin of his feet had known instinctively what lurked in the sand. Something lived there, he'd certainly fathomed that, but not whether it posed a threat to humans. Trusting his own body's hunch, interpreting it, Tatsuro concluded that the countless snakes shimmering up from the seabed had to be poisonous. Only that could explain why his nerves had been so on edge.

His strength helplessly drained from his body, and not because he was letting it go limp. He remembered all too well. Just before reaching the island, when he was about to swim off the sandbar across deeper water, he'd felt a sharp pain at the tip of his left foot. When he'd sat cross-legged on the pier to inspect it, there had been two tiny red perforations at the base of his toe.

I was bitten by a sea snake.

Even as the thought dawned on Tatsuro, it somehow didn't seem real. It wasn't that the snake's venom was finally beginning to take effect. Rather, what was sucking the strength from his body was the very realization that he'd been bitten. Slowly, he drifted with the tide. Sometimes face up, sometimes face down, alternating his gaze between the highway and the opposite horizon, he wafted on the surface. Everything seemed somber, hushed. He couldn't even hear the sound the water made when he turned his body. Running parallel to the highway, the horizon seemed like the great beyond. By contrast, the highway and the occasional cars that streamed past were clearly of this world. In that case, what did the island hovering between the two signify? A relay point between this world and the next?

Floating on his back, Tatsuro took slow breaths. With his ears underwater and his chin slightly turned up, he could fill his lungs with plenty of air. He felt, however, an unpleasant ticklishness all along his nether side. The snakes stretching up from the ocean floor didn't actually reach him, but as if red tongues were licking his back, discomfort spread from there all across his body.

The silence that enveloped him was eerie. Why didn't he feel more panicked? The man who was breathing calmly in and out seemed like someone other than himself to Tatsuro. He wondered why human beings feared snakes. Did our distant ancestors' terror of reptiles, especially of dinosaurs, linger in our species' collective memory? No, that wasn't it. Taking a cue from the two intertwined black snakes he'd just seen, Tatsuro arrived at the answer.

The double helixes of DNA that comprise our genes.

A photographed replica he'd seen showed cellular DNA as two intertwining threads, joined by base pairs, spiraling heavenward. The picture hadn't made him associate the double helix with snakes. Yet, just now, glimpsing sea snakes stretching up from the seabed, he'd instinctively thought of DNA. It occurred to him then that humanity's deep-rooted fear of snakes was an effect of our awe and fear for that which dominated individual organisms since the dawn of life.

People have an unconscious understanding of the workings of the universe. We also instinctively know the microscopic world—our cells' makeup, even the atom's structure. Science is only powerful when it elucidates what we already vaguely comprehend.

That was another thing Tatsuro's wife had said.

He felt bound. A single chromosome chain had divided meiotically from his wife's reproductive cells and intertwined with a strand from his own cells to bring their son and their daughter into the world. His son was dead, but his daughter was walking along the highway at the same pace as her drifting father and yelling at him.

"Papa!"

It was then that her voice reached his ears. At the same instant, saltwater rushed into his throat, sending him into a fit of violent coughing. He lifted his face from the water and took a breath. It was like poking his head into another world. Suddenly, he could hear the gurgling of water he hadn't been registering until then. The shift resembled the way gulping down saliva restored equilibrium to his eardrums after a painful change in air pressure. With a loud pop deep in his ears, the world changed dramatically as if on cue, the quietude banished far away.

Tatsuro's arms and legs churned the sea's surface, and he saw water bubbles that had been sinking down bob back upwards. He struggled like mad.

"Papa!" his daughter was screaming.

When he looked in the direction of her voice, her expression was fraught. His daughter—all alone on the highway, unable to drive or speak the language, suitcase-less. The sole inheritor of his chromosomes was calling out to him. He let his tingling left foot go limp and managed to stay afloat with only the slow movements of his arms.

As soon as he got out of the water, he sat down on a rock and gasped violently. His pulse was probably close to 200 bpm. The tremors that arose from every cell in his body resonated and syncopated with the rhythm of his heartbeat.

That was close.

He had been on the verge of crossing over to the other side. Tatsuro didn't fear death, but his body trembled uncontrollably at the thought of leaving his daughter behind to fend for herself.

His left foot was still numb. He stretched the leg and rubbed around the knee. Yuko was crouching right by his straightened leg. Her eyes welling with tears, her face red with agitation, she was coughing up sobs.

"Oh, Papa, please…" she said simply, fixing him with a reproachful glare. Her anger and fear had yet to subside.

Tatsuro placed a hand on her shoulder and stood up, but when he tried to walk he was overcome by vertigo. His vision grew dark and he felt like throwing up. His stomach was full of the seawater he'd swallowed. He closed both eyes and bent over, hands on knees, and waited for the feeling to pass. Still in the same posture, he glanced at his watch.

Just fifteen minutes.

It had been 2:15 p.m. when he'd pulled the car over and set out for the island. Now it was exactly 2:30. Only fifteen minutes had elapsed. It simply didn't add up. There was a major discrepancy between the series of rich images burnt into his retinas and that time span. In particular, it completely failed to account for the minutes he had spent walking around the island.

Since he had swum around the sandbar, they were standing quite a bit north of where the car was parked. As he and Yuko walked the distance, over a hundred yards, Tatsuro tried to make sense of what had happened to him. But no—referencing a third-person view beat trying to make sense of his own actions.

What could it have looked like to Yuko?

"Tell me what you saw." It was a strange question.

Just tell me, honestly, what you saw.

Tatsuro was afraid of the answer. Somehow he sensed that there was a gap between what he'd experienced and the reality Yuko had witnessed.

"Oh, Papa, please!"

She'd said that often ever since she was little. *Oh, Papa, please…* Whenever she was dissatisfied with him, she prefaced her complaints with those words.

"Papa, please, you can't drown!"

Gradually that spot, where Tatsuro had nearly drowned, came into view. Yuko seemed to resent the deep green water that swirled just in front of the pier, the dark hues that had nearly stolen away her father. But Tatsuro's gaze rested elsewhere. He was looking at the pier beyond. To be exact, he was searching for the fishing boat that should have been tied to it. It was nowhere to be seen. Wondering if they'd set out again, he scanned the sea but found no sign of it.

The pier, now that he gazed upon it anew, wasn't sturdy enough for mooring. Parts of it were rotten and falling away. It didn't even look strong enough to support the weight of a person.

"That fishing boat…" Tatsuro started to ask, but bit back his words.

"Huh?" Yuko looked at him. "What fishing boat?"

"Never mind." Tatsuro fell silent. He didn't need to ask.

Yuko hadn't seen any boat, not one bit of it, moored to the pier. He changed his line of questioning. "Did I almost drown out there?"

He pointed towards the deep water just in front of the sandbar, and Yuko nodded yes.

"And then what?"

His daughter frowned and peered into his face. "Oh, no. You mean you don't remember?"

"Just tell me."

Using a lot of gestures, Yuko described in detail what she had seen. Apparently, Tatsuro had foundered as he'd swum into the deeper waters between the sandbar and the island.

Makes sense. Right after I felt the pain in my left foot.

Tatsuro had gone under and failed to surface for several moments. When he finally re-emerged, he had drifted a little north, parallel to the highway. He floated quietly, without moving his limbs, letting the tide carry him. Screaming all the while, Yuko followed her slowly drifting father along the shore. "Papa!" she called over and over, wrestling with the terror of abandonment, desperately trying to wake him up. Perhaps she'd succeeded because her father did come to, sinking below once more, spitting water, and clumsily beginning to swim again. From the end of the shoal he had swum towards the highway, arriving ashore more than a hundred yards north of the car.

It felt strange hearing another person describe his own actions to him. Just as he had suspected, the time he'd spent on the island was unaccounted for. Everything had been so colorful, so striking, yet it had not been real.

There was only one possible explanation: the sandbar was a nest of sea snakes, and one of them had bitten his left foot. Sea snakes had some venom that assailed humans' central nervous system. Poisoned, Tatsuro had dreamily drifted with the current, wafting at the frontier between seawater and air, hallucinating that he was on the island.

A hallucination.

When he confirmed that fact, the steam-powered railway carriage and the feel of the iron rails came back vividly.

That was a hallucination?

The faucet that spouted water, the fishing boat that moored at the pier, the comforting warmth radiated by the islanders who came ashore. All of it had the touch of reality. All that had been a hallucination? It was hard to accept. With a loud sound something had changed. Fatigue gnawed at his very core.

Taking a better look at the island, Tatsuro saw now that it wasn't large enough to support a settlement or a train. At the same time, he sensed it: the other side gliding toward his. This was how he had to live. A perilous path—the fragile passage over which this side and the other overlapped never led to utopia.

Finally Tatsuro grasped why he'd felt a compulsion to cross over to the island. He'd harbored the drive unconsciously ever since his wife and his son had died in an accident. A longing to cross over to the other side. His shattered family would never be made whole. The fishing boat coming home to the island—it had transformed the crumbling village into a bright place. Over the past six years, how many times had he dreamt that? A wish for restoration that slumbered deep in his heart and that never went away must have manifested as an illusory fishing boat.

As he started the engine, still-hot air came blowing out of the vents in the dashboard. In the passenger's seat, Tatsuro's daughter was chanting under her breath with both eyes squeezed shut. Whenever they visited the family grave, she always shut her eyes tight and offered a prayer like this. Tatsuro had never asked her what she was praying for.

"Our suitcase will be back, won't it?" she asked abruptly.

His girl was probably right. The suitcase they'd transported to another terminal had to be back in Miami by now.

Beyond the Darkness

1

Through the camera's viewfinder, Yoshiaki's fair-skinned face looked out of focus against the brand-new wallpaper. Hesitant to press the shutter, Eriko lowered the camera.

"Should I use the flash?" she asked Yoshiaki, who posed leaning against the wall.

The pale walls and floors emitted that new-house smell. It was the middle of March, the season when days grow longer. There was no direct sunlight, but the spanking newness of the house made the space almost overly bright. Through the viewfinder, though, it looked like there wasn't enough light.

"No, you don't need any flash," Yoshiaki muttered, relaxed his pose, and refolded his arms.

"What?" Eriko asked, cupping her hand behind her ear. Given the context, she shouldn't have needed him to repeat himself.

"Just take it already," Yoshiaki said. He ditched his pose, leaned his head against the wall in a more natural manner, and sighed. He was thoroughly exhausted from unpacking after their move. It was a struggle just to maintain a stance.

"Here we go."

After the shutter snapped, the film automatically advanced to the next frame.

"Now it's your turn," Yoshiaki prompted.

He stood Eriko in front of the full-service kitchen and placed his hands on her shoulders to turn her sideways. Then he took a few steps back and peered through the viewfinder, focusing on her protruding belly. He desperately wanted a photograph of the baby, who was arriving in about a month, while it was still in its mother's womb. Yoshiaki, who turned thirty-one that year, had never seen a photo of his mother when she was pregnant with him. There were many pictures of him after he was born but not a single one of his mother in her final trimester. To him, it seemed that no other image deserved to be preserved more. Held up in front of a mirror, an infant, at only a few months old, could see its own face. Yet there was no way for a fetus holding its knees inside a womb to see the mother from the outside. It wasn't an external shot per se but the mother's expression as she carried the baby that needed to be seen.

"Smile, smile!"

There's something almost laughable about the profile of a near-to-term woman. Bulging out her belly and keeping her shoulders back, Eriko rested lightly against the edge of the sink to stop herself from falling over. She put her hands under her belly and pretended to lift it up for a unique pose.

Yoshiaki pressed the shutter, set the flash, moved a few steps to the side, and pressed the shutter again. Stunned by the flash, Eriko blinked.

"Enough, let's go to the bedroom," she said, less miffed

about having blinked than about having two shots taken in the same pose.

The couple moved to the bedroom, the living room, and to the foyer, alternating between model and photographer. It felt like they had taken lots of photos, but the camera's indicator pointed between 12 and 14.

"What should we do?" Eriko asked.

They had planned to finish the roll, but only a third of the 36-exposure film was used, and she couldn't help but feel they were being wasteful.

"I guess we can't finish it. But that's okay, we'll just keep it. We'll use it a lot anyway after this one's born," Yoshiaki said as he gently patted his wife's stomach.

"That's true."

The couple looked relieved that they'd arrived at the same conclusion.

Purchasing their new house had been quite a stretch. Noticing that the price tag was impacting trivial matters and mentioning the fact carelessly were two different things.

Moving from a one-bedroom apartment in Naka Meguro to a condo in the suburbs involved additional monthly expenses of tens of thousands of yen. "If the monthly cost is about the same as what you're paying as rent, you'll be better off taking out a mortgage and buying since that way it'll remain as an asset," the couple had been seduced at every turn by realtors. Even so, if this were just two years ago, such a purchase would have been impossible. Although they'd nearly given up on the dream of owning a home, they decided to purchase this place just half a year ago, their desires rekindled by rampant rumors that prices had bottomed out. They readied ten million yen for a down payment and looked for a house with a mortgage comparable to their current rent, but all the places that met their requirements were far from the metropolitan area. They had to choose between upping their mortgage and a longer commute. They'd agreed on a shorter commute and closed on the house three months ago.

It was their first weekend in their new home. Yoshiaki had taken a day off from work for the day of the move, but his heavily pregnant wife couldn't be expected to unpack on her own. There'd been nothing they could do but to leave the majority of their belongings boxed up for three days. They got to work the first thing Saturday morning, and now with all the cardboard boxes gone, they deemed it a perfect opportunity to take pictures of their shiny new home. But after using a third of the 36 exposures, the word "thrift" occurred to the couple simultaneously, and they couldn't snap the shutter anymore.

One month later, though, they had their newborn daughter to use the remaining film on. The baby was born slightly underweight at just 5 lbs. 12 oz., even though Yoshiaki was a solidly built man, while her face clearly resembled his. After a weeklong stay in the hospital, mother and daughter returned to their new home, and the leftover film was finally expended. The new home and the newborn included on the same roll looked all the more vibrant given that it was now April, springtime.

The family portrait of the Fukazawa family, Yoshiaki, Eriko, and the new member, Aya, was freshness itself. They were content in every way. The new home may have cost them dearly, but the inestimable emotional comfort was worth it. Just five minutes to the station via bus or twenty minutes on foot, the location was satisfactory, and the quiet residential neighborhood was ideal. Their apartment was on the eastern side of the third floor of a seven-story condominium and had three bedrooms, a living room, a dining room, and a kitchen. They had a decent view, any sounds from their neighbors were almost entirely muffled, and compared to their former rickety apartment on the first floor, it was a good deal more cushy. They could even hear birdsong in the mornings. Although the trek into the city had increased by half an hour, overall their gains outweighed their losses.

"We could live here forever," Yoshiaki and Eriko told each other.

2

The phone rang almost the instant the baby fell asleep. Eriko put up the bars to keep her daughter from rolling over and falling out of the crib and left the bedroom quietly. There was still steam in the hallway from the bathroom. She'd been bathing with Aya in her arms only just now and run into the bedroom without even drying herself off properly.

The ringing of the phone coaxed her to hurry. She had to slip quietly into the living room and lift the receiver to avoid waking up the baby. It must have already rung about seven, eight times. Eriko opened the living room door, and relying on only the faint light that spilled in to guide her, picked up the phone, panting, and answered: "Hello?" She thought it must be her husband so she'd used a flat, casual tone. She reached to turn on the living room light, but with the receiver pressed to her ear, she couldn't reach the switch. Standing in the dimness she said "hello" again, louder this time, trying to elicit a response from the caller.

There was no answer. It was too dark to see the clock's hands, but estimating from the time she'd bathed, it must have been shortly after 9:00 p.m. The other end of the line remained silent.

With calls from a public phone, sometimes the other party couldn't be heard at all due to a faulty connection. Eriko raised her voice further. "Hello, can't you hear me?"

Still no answer.

"Weird." She was just about to replace the receiver when she heard a man's voice.

"You should've told me you were moving."

He spoke with a lisp and had poor enunciation, but that's what Eriko thought she heard.

She held her breath. There was a quiet cackle on the other end of the line. She slammed the receiver and held it down in place with both hands. The subdued laughter seemed to linger in the air. She thought if she were to let go of the phone the voice would revive.

Once sure that nothing was about to happen, Eriko walked away from the phone and went to turn on all the lights until the living room was fully bright. She pulled down the window blinds, looked around the room, and rubbed at her upper arms with her hands, feeling a chill. Although it was mid-May and the air in the room was quite temperate, the voice had left a cold sensation on her skin. The man's words still rang in her mind.

You should've told me you were moving.

Eriko replayed the words endlessly in her head as she

paced back and forth from the table.

The phone was ringing again. It had already rung twice, but Eriko hadn't noticed. Like a siren far in the distance, it sounded anxious. When the third ring reached her ears, Eriko finally grabbed the receiver. Already having forgotten the voice of the man, with a wan face and heart she put the phone to her ear and stood in silence.

"Is our baby already asleep?"

Eriko's nerves immediately thawed. As the tension in her body uncoiled she sank to the floor. She managed to ask in a strangled voice, "Honey, where are you now?"

"At the station."

Eriko switched the receiver from her right ear to her left. Something lodged deep in her ear was making it hard to hear clearly. "Which one?"

"I should be able to see you and our baby's sleeping face in about ten minutes."

"Come home quickly."

"Do you want anything?"

"No, just get home as fast as possible."

"Sure."

Eriko sat in a daze for a while after hanging up. She checked the clock every ten seconds and imagined where her husband was at each moment and repeatedly checked the bedroom as she kept thinking that she'd heard the baby crying.

Turning on the TV, she flipped through the channels but couldn't find anything that held her interest. Her mind was restless. The final scores of the night's ballgames were being announced. She thought she was paying attention but retained no memory of whether her favorite team had won.

Her awareness was moving in a completely different direction.

Thinking to warm up some milk she opened the fridge, and that's when the doorbell rang.

"Coming!"

Eriko closed the fridge and turned around. Her husband must have arrived at last.

3

After taking his shoes off at the entryway, Yoshiaki took off his tie and handed it to Eriko.

"Hey, there was a phone call just a while ago." Eriko gripped the tie in front of her chest, demonstrating that she was eager for him to listen. She tried to block him from leaving the foyer.

"Hold on a second," Yoshiaki whispered into her ear softly and went to the bedroom to check on his daughter first. He opened the door but didn't step inside, and satisfied to hear his daughter sleeping, turned his attention back to Eriko. "So, what about this call?"

"Come." Eriko pushed her husband's back all the way into the living room and gently closed the door behind them. "Have you had dinner?" she asked in typical fashion, gaining back a measure of composure.

"Yeah, I ate at work. So, what happened?"

Eriko glanced at the dial phone beside her. "He called again."

"Who?"

"It was the same man. No doubt about it."

Yoshiaki thought for a while. He wasn't grasping the drift. "What man?"

"Come on. Remember the prank calls I was getting at our place in Naka Meguro?"

Yoshiaki couldn't be blamed for having only a vague recollection. The calls always came during the day while he was at work, so he'd never answered any of the prank calls himself. When his wife, cowered by the eerie voice on the other end, had begged him to do something, he'd told her, "Leave it alone, we're moving soon anyways," and not taken the matter seriously. Had it been more persistent, he might have contacted NTT to get a new number, but there'd been only five or six calls. After the move, their address would change from Tokyo to Kanagawa prefecture, and the chances of the same caller finding them would be slim. Naturally, they didn't sign up to have a prerecorded tape answer callers with their new number, and they passed on a phone book listing.

"Is it really the same guy?" Yoshiaki doubted that point first and foremost. Could a casual prank caller look up a new number so easily?

"I'm sure of it. He even said, 'You should've told me you were moving,'" Eriko replied imitating the man's tone. Mimicking him seemed to bring the man who lurked behind the receiver closer to her. Terrified, she pressed a hand to her mouth and fell silent.

"Strange." Yoshiaki looked up to the ceiling and considered the ways a total stranger might look up a new phone number from an old one. He searched his memory. Before sending out postcards with their new address to friends and acquaintances, he'd called his closest associates directly to notify them of their new number. He remembered every single person—just five guys whom he considered his best friends. His business card was printed with his office phone number with no mention of private info. It had only been two months since they moved, and his high school and college alumni directory still listed his old address.

"Did the voice sound familiar?"

Eriko shook her head, hand still pressed to her mouth.

"Think carefully. Someone you know could be the one harassing you."

It would make sense if it were a friend of a friend whose voice she didn't remember all that well. The man might have subtly asked a mutual acquaintance for her number. The idea that one of the people they'd notified of their move had done it didn't enter his mind even for a second.

"What do you think?" Yoshiaki urged.

Eriko, who'd been puffing out her right cheek, turned her head slightly and asked, "What?"

"What do you mean, 'What?' Weren't you listening?"

It seemed to him that rather than not hearing him, she'd been too preoccupied for his words to get through. When he stuck his face closer to her with a dismayed expression, her own face contorted as if she were ready to burst into tears. Her right temple was twitching. The skin between her eyebrows was creased and the worry written around her eyes and mouth distorted her entire face. Some shorter strands of her shoulder-length hair curled upwards as if to symbolize her frayed nerves.

"I'm sorry, can you say that again? I couldn't hear you very well."

"The guy that called," Yoshiaki said more loudly, "might be a friend of a friend or something. That's what I said."

Eriko's eyes went wide with surprise. "I don't know," she said, her voice nasal. Sticking her index finger into her right ear, she wiggled it around and swallowed.

"Is something wrong?"

"You know how you get that tight feeling in your ears when there's a change in air pressure? My ear sorta feels like that." Eriko swallowed again and pressed down on the base of her nose.

"Anyway, let's just see what happens for now," Yoshiaki concluded indifferently, putting an end to the conversation. Glancing sidelong at Eriko, who kept fiddling with her nose and ears, he unbuttoned his shirt.

4

On the first Monday of June, Eriko got the second prank call since moving. It came slightly earlier in the evening right after she'd done the dishes. Aya slept on a flat Japanese-style cushion on the floor, and Yoshiaki was working late at the office as usual.

Once she knew it was the same man, she resisted hanging up right away and mentally readied herself to sound out the caller.

"You're alone now, aren't you?" The question came with wet noises as if the man were smacking his lips as he spoke.

Eriko nearly lost the willpower to keep holding up

the receiver. Even over the phone, conversing with an utterly malicious person took courage. In Eriko's case, it took her at least ten seconds to work up a reply.

"You're the one who used to called me. How did you get this number?"

The man's sloppy laughter welled up through the receiver. Eriko pictured a mad, drooling dog infected with rabies. "Of course I know the number. I'm not stupid."

"What do you get out of doing this?" She tried to feign calmness but her voice trembled. She moved the receiver away from her mouth so he wouldn't sense her agitation.

"I can just picture it. Your face as you're ready to burst out crying…"

Her throat was parched. She tried to speak, but the back of her throat was bone dry, turning her voice husky. She frantically rifled through her memory. Could he be an acquaintance, or someone who held a grudge against her? Nobody came to mind. She closed her eyes and tried to think of who might have a similar voice, but her mind ran into darkness. Something faintly tangible seemed to lie within that darkness but she couldn't trawl it in.

"I'm calling the police," Eriko managed to squeeze out.

"Pointless. You don't even know who I am. Eh? Or do you?"

Intense resentment engulfed Eriko. The man was lobbing threatening words from deep in the darkness where he hid out of reach. She couldn't tolerate the unfairness, the informational imbalance.

With a voice pitched high with anger, her face ready to crumple into tears, Eriko pointed out that she didn't live alone: "Coward. Next time, why don't you call when my husband's home?"

"Your husband?" piped the man. *So what,* his tone seemed to say.

Eriko's anger and terror subsided just a bit when she pictured her husband. *If only he were here...* She believed her husband could confront the caller and browbeat him into silence even over the phone. Her husband was not a slender man.

"That pasty dweeb?"

"Huh?" Eriko felt her whole body stiffen. Although her husband had a stout built, he was fair-skinned and didn't sport much body hair. She was afraid that the man was referring to those characteristics when he said "pasty."

"You're impressive, doing it with a guy like that. How many pregnancies does this make anyway?"

Eriko was struck dumb. Still, she glanced towards her baby sleeping on a cushion right before her. That he seemed to know she'd just given birth was uncanny, but why did he ask how many times she'd been pregnant? In her twenty-nine years, of course this had been her only pregnancy.

"Hey, now, why're you so quiet?" He wasn't pressing her for an answer. The peeved, languid delivery sounded theatrical.

Eriko's mind was in disarray. She could almost put her finger on whatever was hidden in the darkness of her memory, but as soon as she managed to touch it she was forcefully repelled.

"You're pretending you can't hear me again, aren't ya."

A chill raced through Eriko's body.

"I know you can hear me. I can tell when someone's ly—"

Eriko slammed the receiver down with instinctive alacrity. Immediately after, she heard a strange ringing inside her ear. She had a hard time hearing the TV that she'd left on, as if the volume had been turned down a notch. She swallowed repeatedly, but it didn't make any difference. She clapped both hands to her ears and sank to the floor.

She didn't have the energy to get back up. Was she suffering from anemia? She thought she saw the lights in the room grow dimmer. The whiteness of the cushion on the floor floated indistinctly across her retinas, and everything seemed to dissolve except for her baby asleep on that cushion. She felt like she'd experienced similar symptoms long ago but shook off the memories from that time. Her heart was racing and she couldn't stop trembling.

For about ten minutes, she had no choice but to sit there with her back against the wall until her hearing and vision returned to normal.

The next day, Yoshiaki stopped by a discount shop on his way back from work to purchase an answering machine. It was obvious that Eriko was having a nervous breakdown, and he needed to put a stop to the prank calls immediately. Ever since they'd gotten married she had the tendency to ask him to repeat himself, but since last night she'd been experiencing a temporary hearing impairment, to the point where even ordinary conversation was difficult. The psychological damage inflicted seemed excessive, but there was no doubt as to the prank calls being the cause. There'd been too few of them to bother consulting with NTT, and the police certainly wouldn't lift a finger. The situation demanded a swift countermeasure, and procuring an answering machine, however makeshift, was it. Setting the machine to "on" at all times removed the risk of unwanted calls. It was the simplest safeguard.

If it weren't for the prank calls he wouldn't have made such a purchase, and his foul mood persisted even as he brought the machine home and set it up. Already shouldering a mortgage incommensurate to their means, their family budget was hardly impervious to this hit of a few ten-thousand-yen bills.

Yoshiaki recorded the outgoing message in his voice.

"Hello, this is the Fukazawa residence. We cannot take your call right now. Please leave your name and a message after the beep."

Most people hung up without leaving a message when they realized no one was home. This meant he needed to let friends and acquaintances know that the machine would be on "away" all the time. That way, Yoshiaki and his wife would avoid missing too many calls from friends.

He set the machine to trigger after five rings. Eriko would have to stand by the phone for that interval without picking up. The tape would then play the greeting and beep. At that point callers could state their name, and their voice would be projected through the speaker. Whether to take the call or not could wait until then. If the caller failed to give a name or was someone she didn't want to speak to, the receiver could just stay put. After a minute of recording, the machine automatically disconnected. She only had to pick up if she wanted to.

Done with the setup, Yoshiaki said, as if to convince himself, "This oughta make the pervert give up." He figured the caller was attempting to satisfy his sexual needs. Eriko's voice over the phone was indeed very charming.

Nonetheless Eriko, who was next to him, still looked ill at ease. To her, the prank caller's motive was totally unfathomable. At the very least she was sure that sexual release wasn't the motive. The boundless malice in the depths of his voice told her otherwise.

5

Towards the middle of June, the Kanto region entered the rain season. Many people disliked the humidity, but it was Yoshiaki's favorite time of the year. The sun, at the largest size it would be all year, peeked through in the breaks between squalls, giving everything he saw a crisp, vivid outline. He loved the sight of the world after the air had been cleansed by rainfall.

The precipitation had let up late in the afternoon that day, the rifts in the clouds rapidly growing larger.

It had been quite some time since Yoshiaki was able to walk through the shopping strip to Tamachi station while there was still plenty of daylight left. Most of the time, he didn't get home until between nine and ten, and having dinner at home was limited to the weekends. Yet at his current pace he'd likely be home by half past seven.

Right before heading down the stairs to the subway platform, he phoned home. After it rang five times, the machine automatically switched on and he heard his voice on the outgoing message.

"Hello, this is the Fukazawa residence…"

No matter how many times he heard the recording, it still felt uncomfortable.

"Eriko, are you listening? It's me, Yoshiaki," he shouted into the mouthpiece not waiting for the message to finish.

There was a click as she picked up. "Hello, honey?"

"It's me. I'm on my way home. I'll have dinner at home tonight," Yoshiaki said slowly and loudly. Eriko's ears were still acting up.

"Great. Come home soon, I need you to listen to something."

"What is it?"

"I can't do it over the phone."

"All right. I'll be back in an hour."

Yoshiaki hung up.

As he stood by the apartment door and looked westward from the edge of the building's exposed corridor, he could still see traces of sunlight. He dreamed of a less hectic life, of how happy he'd be if he could come home at this hour every day. Burdened with a 25-year mortgage, however, quitting his current job at a major insurance company to find other work was, realistically speaking, an impossibility. He'd been able to purchase his own home only thanks to his decent salary. As for the home, sparkling new and spacious, it gave them greater satisfaction than they'd anticipated. To wish for further luxury would be a sin...

The doorbell rang out its ever-satisfying chime. As soon as the door opened to reveal half of his wife's head peeking through, he could hear his daughter crying in the living room.

"Welcome home." Eriko looked haggard.

"Our little baby is crying."

The infant's cries tumbled out from behind the living room door at the end of the hallway. Yoshiaki kicked his shoes off, ran inside, and got onto all fours, putting his face close to the baby's. Her wrinkly, small face was contorted and bright red. The baby showed no signs of stopping her wails even though Yoshiaki brushed his cheek against hers.

"It's fine, she's just hungry." Eriko loosened her skirt, and after pulling an arm free from her t-shirt, she scooped up the baby from the side and walked to the living-room door.

"While I'm nursing her, can you please listen to that?" Eriko asked, thrusting her chin towards the phone.

"The answering machine?"

"I just… I'm fed up with this," she muttered weakly, then stepped into the hallway and closed the door. It seemed like she didn't ever want to hear the message again and was using breastfeeding as a pretext to leave the room.

Yoshiaki played the recording and heard the prank caller's voice for himself for the first time. The man started speaking as if to interrupt the greeting, before it was finished.

"Pfft, an answering machine? Don't mean a thing. You're probably right there listening, aren't ya. To my voice." The man's tone rose. "Hey, are you listening to me? Hello, hello? You can probably hear my voice better this way, eh? Yo, ugly, you listening? Pig! You lewd slut! You haven't changed one bit."

Yoshiaki trembled to hear such filthy abuse hurled at his wife. He was far more enraged than if he himself had been badmouthed to his face. His wife wasn't ugly, a pig, nor a lewd slut. Emphatically rejecting the calumny, and seized with naked hostility for the man, he punched the floor with his fist.

The voice droned on. "Still keeping mum? Please, pick up the phone. 'Nuff pretendin' you can't hear me..."

The message ended there. Reining in his temper, Yoshiaki listened to the message again from the beginning. Something bothered him. Hearing that line, *You haven't changed one bit,* Yoshiaki couldn't help thinking that the man was an old acquaintance of his wife's. Was some guy she'd been seeing before she got married harassing her now? Yoshiaki had married Eriko three years ago. Back then, at twenty-six, she had been a virgin. That fact was certain. Even now, in Yoshiaki's eyes, Eriko was far from lewd and decidedly no slut. In fact, he knew of no other woman whom the old-fashioned word "chaste" suited so well. But if she'd developed a relationship with another man after their marriage and had come across as lewd to him... A tawdry scenario, like something out of a soap opera, flashed across Yoshiaki's mind and vanished just as quickly. It was obvious from his wife asking him to listen to the tape and going to the next room to breastfeed the baby. Exposing her husband to the voice of a partner in adultery ran counter to common sense.

He peeked into the other room and found Eriko faced away from the door and breastfeeding in the gloom with only the midget lamp on. Yoshiaki approached her from behind, put his hand on her shoulder, and whispered, "I listened to it."

Eriko sniffled a few times as she rocked gently to and fro. He could sense that she was on the verge of tears just from the hunch of her spine.

"I'm fed up," she repeated.

Was she feeling like throwing in the towel, the joy of owning a home halved thanks to prank calls that came in quick succession, just when they were getting settled into a new neighborhood as a family of three? Taking out an over-ambitious mortgage and increasing his commute to work was worth it if it benefited his wife and child. The man's voice had trespassed and polluted their first steps towards a life of contentment. Yoshiaki brimmed with a different strain of anger.

"The bastard… You really can't think of anyone?"

Eriko, still facing away, shook her head. "I have no idea."

In truth she probably didn't. Yet she seemed troubled by the man's insinuations that he knew her. Some fellow nursing a persistent grudge towards her over something trivial wasn't out of the question. If, by any chance, she'd incurred ill will from some passing man, then remembering him would be a herculean task.

"Think about it some. If we know who it is, we can figure out a way to deal with him."

The first call had come around February. Yoshiaki tried recalling Eriko's activities during January and February when they still lived in the Naka Meguro apartment. At the end of the preceding year she'd left the university hospital where she'd worked as a nutritionist to nest at home, eager to prepare for their daughter's birth. Never a fan of parading around, Eriko's sphere of activity was particularly limited during that period.

"Why always me… just me?" she demanded, her voice turning weepy mid-sentence.

Yoshiaki moved his hand resting on her shoulder up and down, caressing her back. He didn't know what else to do. What could he do to alleviate his wife's anxiety? The infant nursing at her nipple made suckling sounds with her lips.

Once again, Yoshiaki was seized with the urge to drag the man behind the voice right through the phone.

6

Eriko did the dishes with the baby strapped to her back. It was just past 7:00 p.m., and NHK News was reporting on a trifling quarrel between apartment building neighbors that had developed into a full-blown murder case. Through the narrow window above the sink, she could look right down onto the rain-drenched roof of a nearby house. From it often issued a shout-fest between a mother and her daughter. As the mother tried to force study or piano practice on her recalcitrant junior or senior high daughter, the emotional tension ratcheted up high enough to be felt in the Fukazawas' apartment as well. Now too Eriko could hear them arguing hysterically, but the muffling rain kept the exact point of contention from leaking out of their home.

The baby had fallen asleep on her back. When Eriko turned her head, she could feel her daughter's soft hair against her cheek.

Suddenly the phone trilled. As soon as Eriko heard the sound, she reflexively looked at the clock. It felt too early for her husband to call. He normally did just shy of nine.

As the number of rings rose, Eriko felt herself stiffen. The noise of the TV and the yelling from next door faded into the background and her mind zeroed in on the ringing phone, her hands stilling on the dishes. After the fifth ring and

Yoshiaki's prerecorded greeting, she heard that man's voice.

"Ugh, not again…" She wanted to yank the cord out of the phone but recalled what Yoshiaki had said: *If we know who it is, we can figure out a way to deal with him.* There might be a clue hidden in the caller's words that could help pin down his identity, so she endured the man's voice as it entered her ear.

"Hey, pig. What're you doing? I know you can hear me. From right there. Don't pretend you can't hear me…"

Eriko felt as though the man had physically trespassed into their home. She was too terrified to even turn around to check. Right by the living room entrance, near the phone stand… The man had snuck all the way into that corner.

"Cut the shit, idiot. Just seeing you pisses me off. What're you doing now? Bathing your brat in a washtub? Or is the munchkin asleep on the cushion? With that stuffed bunny next to it and in that stupid little vest? I'll smash everything. Who do you think you are…"

The tape ran out there, ending the call automatically. It took a while for the man's words to register in Eriko's mind.

Bathing in a washtub… Indeed, that afternoon she had bathed the baby using a pink plastic washtub. *Asleep on the cushion…* Afterwards, she usually put the baby down for a nap—placing a white cushion and covering it with a bath towel. She always put a stuffed animal beside the baby. The bunny was her daughter's especial favorite. She didn't remember putting a vest on her daughter today, but they did have one that Eriko's mother had made, with an appliqué of a cat on the chest…

How could the man know all this?

Eriko slammed shut the narrow window above the kitchen sink. Her heart was pounding. The living room was on the building's corner with windows on the eastern and northern sides. She ran over and lowered the blinds one by one, changed the channel on the TV, and turned up the volume. That brief spurt of activity was enough to make her gasp for air. She found it difficult to stay standing so she perched on the sofa and stared at the ceiling for a while in blank amazement.

Someone was watching! There was no other explanation. The room was being observed from outside.

Was it being watched now? Eriko got up and went to the blinds she'd just pulled closed and peeked through to check outside. As she already knew, no other buildings more than three stories tall existed within several hundred yards. Peering into their third-floor apartment and seeing their baby napping called for a building with at least four stories. To the east and the north, there was only one that fit the description. The public housing project to the northeast had seven floors, the same as their building. There was simply no other in sight.

Even at this hour, there were no lights on in the project. Eriko doubted whether anyone actually lived there. What if it was an abandoned building? As soon as that thought came to her, her ears started to ring. She pulled at her earlobes and swallowed, but the discomfort behind her eardrums didn't disappear. The man's voice, burned into her ears, began to lose that unique human timber. Somehow, it ceased to feel like any living person's. Against her will, her imagination careened towards the worst. Getting a peep of their family life, a picture of bliss, ghosts dwelling on the top floor of that abandoned project saw fit to make prank calls and... Images like that invaded her mind. Maybe the man was ensconced in another dimension and was using a phone line to castigate her. Perhaps he'd snuck into the living room to whisper directly into her ear...

The baby sling was biting into her shoulders and her collarbones ached. Eriko's knees dissolved, and she sank to the floor and trembled with terror. Her hands, with which she covered her face, became drenched in tears. What she couldn't stand was that the new home they'd sacrificed so much to acquire seemed jinxed. No, she didn't really believe in ghosts. But until a logical explanation put the issue to rest, her terror would only grow entwined with such fantasies. She knew very well from experience that it took years to recover inner peace once she was ensnared by this stuff.

She slumped forward, rubbed her forehead against the floor, and muttered, "Why me... just me... "

Her ears continued to ring. To add insult to injury, the back of her head started to ache dully, and perhaps thanks to that the lights in the room felt a little less bright.

7

As he listened to the messages over and over, Yoshiaki began to think that Eriko's worries were not groundless.

The prank caller did seem privy to the Fukazawas' everyday life as if he were witnessing it. But on second thought, most any family with a two-month-old baby would bathe their baby in a washtub, put her down to nap on a cushion where her mother could see, give her stuffed animals, and dress her in a handmade vest. A commonsensical list enumerating the activities of a household with an infant necessarily overlapped with the Fukazawas' actual routines. Everybody read guidebooks on childrearing with the arrival of a newborn. Anyone who knew that Yoshiaki and Eriko had a two-month-old baby could easily imagine their daily life.

Just seeing you pisses me off.

That was the line that worried Yoshiaki the most. Unless the culprit were actually viewing her through, say, a telescope, "seeing you" wasn't a phrase he was likely to use on the spur. It would be an extremely unnatural thing for the prank caller to say to someone he had called at random. Upon Eriko's request Yoshiaki had gone to the local housing project to confirm that it was not, in fact, abandoned. If someone were observing their home from the outside, then as Eriko suspected, the upper floors of the project represented the only possibility. Think as he might, no other spots seemed suitable. But if the prank caller was a resident of the project, what of the calls they'd gotten at their old apartment in Naka Meguro? It had all started when they still lived there, and they could hardly explain it away as a coincidence.

Yoshiaki was confounded. Fear tends to skyrocket when no logical explanation offers itself. He feigned calm since he was with Eriko, but after running repeatedly into the same questions and realizing he was getting nowhere, his mind conjured up ominous thoughts.

Eriko muttered "police" as if in a daze and said, "We can't live here anymore," as though she wanted them to move again.

Yoshiaki felt blood rush to his head. "We have to move?

Are you kidding? Did you forget how hard it was to get this place?" He knew yelling at her was a misdirection of his rage, but remembering how difficult it had been to scrape together a down payment and all the hardships they'd gone through, his tone got rough. Things had finally begun to settle. He didn't want to go back to square one.

"Well, it's okay for you, since you're at work all day."

Trapped inside almost all day caring for a two-month-old baby, defenseless in face of a Peeping Tom's gaze... Yoshiaki could easily imagine the state of panic he might be in if he were a woman stuck in Eriko's position.

A logical explanation was what they needed. Yoshiaki racked his brains.

"Maybe the bastard was just trying to make you think he's watching, to scare you." It wasn't impossible. Harassment was always an objective for a prank caller. The caller might have implied he'd been watching in order to terrorize her when in fact he didn't even know her address.

"What difference does that make? As long as there's even the slightest chance that he's watching, I'm going to feel hemmed in."

A year ago, Yoshiaki had gone in for a thorough health exam and been told he might have cancer. During the two weeks he'd waited for the results of the re-examination, he'd found himself in the mental state of a cancer patient. *Even the slightest chance...* It was the same. Yoshiaki understood perfectly well what Eriko meant. A makeshift excuse didn't pass muster. The only way to set his wife's mind at ease was to remove the problem in its entirety.

They could speak of hypotheticals forever. Maybe the caller had gotten his info from a friend who had visited them and now spoke as if he'd seen into their apartment. Assuming it was a friend of a friend also solved the mystery of how he'd gotten the number of their new home. Yoshiaki tried to convince himself with this poor excuse of a deduction, but as he did he felt ashamed of himself. He was reminding himself of his father, who only ever half-heartedly replied to his wife even when she was in a fix and needed help. Yoshiaki feared he might end up retreading his father's behavior if he wasn't careful. While his mother had carried the weight of the household on her back, his father simply feigned ignorance. Yoshiaki didn't want to follow in his father's footsteps.

"All right. I'm going to do something about this."

It wasn't that he had a specific plan. All he could do for now was to contact all of his friends who had recently come to visit and subtly question them. In addition, he would determine who, including door-to-door salesmen, even briefly stood in the entryway of their home. Or should he contact the police since a suspicious person might be loitering in the neighborhood?

"Please, I'm so scared." Eriko was still shivering slightly.

"Hey, Eriko, could you list up every single person who's come to the door while I was away at work?"

Eriko took a pen and paper and started to write, stopping now and then to think.

Newspaper salesmen, the NHK fee collector, religious solicitors, the electrician who came to fix the air conditioner, the technician from the phone company… Such designations began to fill the memo pad. Yoshiaki didn't know where to start.

When I find you, you won't get off lightly.

What spurred on Yoshiaki's overworked frame was the hatred he felt for the prank caller who dared to impose such an outrageous burden on him.

8

The next day, he visited the police station in his precinct and told them the gist of the story. The assigned officer listened cordially, but that was as far as it went. It was beyond clear that at this point, there was nothing for the police to act on. The officer offered mere consolation: "We'll step up the neighborhood patrol." Yoshiaki could only respond with a short bow and a thank-you when he left.

For a week afterwards, Yoshiaki used all his spare time even at work desperately attempting to ascertain the identity of the prank caller.

He called friends he had invited over, opened up about the situation, and asked if they had any clues. He also asked a coworker for advice. He came up empty-handed. Regarding the coworker, Yoshiaki was sorely disappointed by his misguided aperçu that Eriko might be having an affair.

On Sunday afternoon, Yoshiaki went to the roof of the municipal housing project and peered into his own apartment with a pair of binoculars, but it was impossible to see what was happening inside. It would take an astronomical telescope to specify types of stuffed animals. Even such a telescope, however, would be helpless against the blind spot from the floor up to a height of about three feet.

From this roof, the visible area was limited to a narrow section of the living room. The baby napped on a cushion on the floor with the stuffed animal right beside her. Yoshiaki couldn't help but feel that this scenario was implausible.

Perhaps a salesman held a terrible grudge, irritated by the way Eriko had spoken to him on the phone. When Yoshiaki answered calls at home, as soon as he figured out it was a solicitation or sales pitch, he'd hang up in a fairly rude manner. Even though it was an inevitable part of their jobs, some callers probably did get upset. When he brought up the possibility to Eriko, she told him she had taken calls from a real estate agent and a securities firm back in Naka Meguro but that she had been polite in declining their offers. As far as Yoshiaki knew, Eriko's phone manners were almost too courteous. It wasn't likely that she'd angered anyone.

Considering the caller phoned both the Naka Meguro apartment and their current place, at one point Yoshiaki suspected their realtor and the moving company. Yet as far as he could remember, there were no issues that would have earned their spite, plus the voice of the prank caller was plainly different. Just to be certain, he called both companies using trumped-up excuses. Both voices that answered were quite unlike the peculiar, lazy speech of the prank caller.

In addition, he checked out by phone the men Eriko had listed: the newspaper salesman, the NHK fee collector, the electrician, the telecom technician... There was no way of knowing the name or number of the religious solicitor, but since Eriko had spoken with him for nearly half an hour, she clearly remembered his speech and there was no need to confirm. She declared there was no way that the solicitor was the prank caller.

By process of elimination, they had crossed off every man on Eriko's list.

Even at work, thoughts of the prank caller plagued Yoshiaki until he was on the verge of a meltdown. Images of the culprit prowling about his neighborhood suddenly assailed him until he gasped for breath and called home worried over the safety of his wife and baby. The nervousness he felt until Eriko picked up the phone… A mere ten seconds sufficed for ghastly scenes to flit through his head. Once he heard his wife's voice, he basked in a moment of relief, but fury soon shot through his body and rendered him incapable of work. He wanted to drag that coward out of the darkness where he hid peeping and consign him to oblivion.

As if his prayers had reached heaven, shortly thereafter Yoshiaki happened across a clue.

Once the calendar turned to July, a heat wave moved in bringing temperatures that reached over 85 degrees for days on end. The end of the rainy season had not been formally announced yet, but for a week there hadn't been a drop of rain.

Running down the stairway in the train station, Yoshiaki felt sweat seeping into the collar of his shirt. He wiped at his neck with his hand and checked his watch. It was just after 9:00 a.m., plenty of time before half past when he had to be at work. His office was less than a ten-minute walk from the JR Tamachi station. He'd left home a little early because he had an errand to run.

After turning right at the shopping strip and walking for a dozen yards he saw the orange sign for Shiba Photo.

Yoshiaki opened the glass door and called to the back.

"Good morning!"

Footsteps sounded down the stairs, and then Kodama, the owner, emerged through the shop curtains. He was a small, old man with gray hair. "Hello," he said.

This was his usual manner of greeting customers. The store was so small it could scarcely hold more than a half-dozen people standing. The darkroom was on the second floor, accessible via the stairs at the rear. Kodama usually worked upstairs and came down only when he heard people in the shop.

"Hot out there, eh?"

"Sure is. It's killing me." With that standard seasonal greeting, Yoshiaki pulled out a finished roll of film from his briefcase.

Kodama slipped on his silver-rimmed glasses and pulled a drawer open. "Baby getting bigger?"

"Indeed."

"Must be pretty cute."

"I guess so."

"Hm? What's the matter? You seem low today."

"Oh, it's nothing…"

Kodama gave him a direct look. "Fukazawa. You look like you've lost weight. Is it the heat?"

"Maybe that too."

"Busy with work?"

Yoshiaki could only give a noncommittal laugh. He had worked part-time at the photo shop for half a year during college. He'd remained friends with Kodama over the ensuing decade. Since the insurance company he worked for was so close by, Yoshiaki had never brought his film anywhere else for ten years. He dropped off his film before work and

121

picked up the finished photos at the end of the day, and through each such occasion, they kept each other updated on their respective lives. After the arrival of the baby, Yoshiaki took up a decidedly larger portion of their conversations. The old man, whose wife had passed away years ago and whose grown son had moved outside of Tokyo for work reasons, by and large found himself in the position of listener.

"No good. You shouldn't work so hard."

Kodama took out an envelope and handed it to Yoshiaki along with a pen.

On the envelope was a form with carbon paper underneath where one could designate a matte or glossy finish, the size of the photograph, etc. Yoshiaki filled it out as usual, checking the boxes. Just as he was about to enter his name and number, his hand stopped moving. Right before him on top of the glass case was a finished roll of 24-exposure film. The small cylinder archived the day-to-day lives of the Fukazawas like a picture scroll. With a newborn in the family, they had wanted to document each and every action of the baby even if it was nothing at all. Such photos naturally included backgrounds and surroundings.

When was the last time I dropped off film?

At the end of the weeklong national holidays in May, he had brought in a roll of 36-exposure film that contained shots of the new house and the newborn. He remembered the composition of most of the pictures, especially the ones of Aya, since he ended up taking most of those. A shot of Aya in a pink washtub being bathed by her mother, Aya's adorable face as she slept on a cushion on the floor… He'd photographed his baby girl's every expression from all possible angles.

And the phone number.

For the last ten years, Yoshiaki had checked the same boxes and entered his phone number and name on envelopes that Kodama had handed him. The last time he'd dropped off film, naturally he had given his new number. Come to think of it, the first prank call to their new home had come right after the May holidays.

Why hadn't he realized it sooner? A photo instantly relayed visual info about the inside of their apartment as if the viewer had actually been inside. The prank caller had divulged no other tidbits in his messages.

The space for his name still blank, Yoshiaki looked up. He desperately tamped down his agitation and assumed an air of nonchalance.

"This film..." he managed before words failed him.

Perplexed, Kodama tilted his head. "What about this film?"

If the system hadn't changed for the last ten years, Kodama only developed black-and-white photos himself and outsourced color processing to a center in the suburbs.

"Hey, what's the problem?" Kodama pressed.

"Who brings these films to the processing center?"

Kodama stood there absentmindedly for a moment, unable to grasp the point of the question. "Who? That would be a man named Hikuma."

"Hikuma? What's his first name?"

"I don't remember. He's a part-timer with Crown Color, so I really don't know much about him."

Shiba Photo and Crown Color had a contract going for more than ten years. Even back when Yoshiaki worked there, a worker from Crown Color came by to pick up the negatives every morning around 9:00 a.m. Back then, it was a university student enrolled in night classes; he collected the undeveloped film from several stores in Minato Ward, took them to the processing center in Nishi Funabashi via the Tozai subway line, and waited for them to be developed. The pictures were ready around 4:00 p.m., and the photographs and negatives had to be returned to each store by five. That way, customers who dropped off their film at 9:00 a.m. could receive their order by after 5:00 p.m. the same day. Color film, including rolls dropped off at convenient stores, were generally processed at locations on the outskirts of Tokyo. All processing centers relied on part-time workers to pick up and return the film and photos. If the delivery person used the subway each way, there was plenty of time to take a look at the developed pictures. And each envelope bore the customer's phone number.

"Since when has this Hikuma person been coming here?"

"Just started this year. I think it was around the beginning of February."

February.

The first prank calls to the Naka Meguro apartment had occurred between February and March.

"What about today?"

"Sorry, he's already come by, so these pictures won't be ready until tomorrow. Is that all right?"

Naturally, the photos wouldn't be ready until the next day if one missed the nine o'clock pick-up.

"Hm? Oh, sure, that's no problem."

There was no rush. Today or tomorrow, as long as he got the photos it was fine, but the fact that he had just missed the prank caller gave Yoshiaki mixed feelings. He wanted to identify the man right then and there, but at the same time he felt a little relieved.

Just seeing you pisses me off.

He could almost hear the man's singular speech echoing in the small shop. Yoshiaki wanted to hear him say the same thing in person to confirm it. Just one word would do. He'd know immediately if he heard that voice again.

"He's coming again at nine tomorrow, right?" Yoshiaki asked to make sure.

"Yeah. He always comes at nine on the dot."

Yoshiaki tried to smile at Kodama but couldn't quite make his face cooperate. A twitch below one eye ruled out any friendly expression. He could tell that the aggravation roiling in his chest was coloring his visage.

"All right, see you later."

He quickly turned away, opened the glass door, and left.

Kodama started to say something, but Yoshiaki pretended not to notice and continued walking towards his office.

Calm down.

His pace quickened as if to match his racing heartbeat, and his sweating noticeably worsened.

9

It was an especially tiring day. Yoshiaki had appointments with three clients from the afternoon into the evening, and by the time he finished up some leftover work at the office, it was already past nine. He declined a colleague's invitation to mahjong, told the section head that he was taking a day off tomorrow, and left for home in a hurry.

He got off the train at Hiyoshi station. Finding he couldn't tolerate his thirst any longer, he bought a can of coffee from a vending machine on the walk home. His building was a stone's throw away. As he drank his coffee, he glanced over to the third floor and checked to see if the lights were on in their apartment. Apparently the curtains were drawn, but no light spilled from between the gaps. His wife and daughter were probably already asleep. Yoshiaki had told Eriko time and again not to stay up waiting for him to return from work.

The space where his wife and daughter slept seemed to float on that corner of the quiet residential area. Yoshiaki finished his coffee, never once taking his eyes off of the corner.

He showered as noiselessly as possible and crawled into the futon laid for him in the Japanese-style room.

His daughter often slept in a crib, but tonight she was breathing evenly next to her mother. Recently, the family of three shared two futons—mom and dad on either side with baby Aya in the middle. It felt right for both Eriko and Yoshiaki.

Though physically drained, having come so close to unveiling the prank caller Yoshiaki was too restless to sleep. He'd taken the following day off from work to check out the lead. What he'd do once he discovered the man was still a question mark, but when he thought of how tortuous the last two months had been, he knew he wouldn't be satisfied without exacting revenge.

Perhaps woken by his turning over, Eriko shifted.

"Welcome home," she whispered right by his ear.

Their daughter slept sucking on her thumb. A short, quiet conversation didn't seem likely to wake her.

"Sorry. Did I wake you?"

"It's fine. I took a nap with her during the day." Eriko laughed, but her "nap" couldn't have been much more than a quick doze at the infant's side.

"Do you know a man named Hikuma?" Despite his reluctance about asking her, the name leapt unchecked from his mouth.

"Hikuma?"

"Yeah."

Eriko tucked the fleece blanket around her hips and repeated the name. "Hikuma, Hikuma..." The room was dim with only a single small bulb lighting the room. The air was humid. "*That* Hikuma?" she exclaimed, her voice colored with surprise.

The length it took for her to remember, the nuance of familiarity... They must have known each other from ages ago.

"You know him?"

There was no answer. Yoshiaki raised his head partway and glanced over at the adjacent futon. Eriko had covered her cheeks with both hands and was staring at the ceiling, her large double-lidded eyes blown even wider.

"Oh, God. It was Hikuma?" Tears fell from her eyes as she spoke.

"Who the hell is he?"

"Hey, are you sure it's Hikuma making those calls?"

"Dammit, who is he?"

"Ah ha, I see... That's why..."

Between them, the baby moved in her sleep. Yoshiaki and Eriko both held their breaths and fell silent. They hadn't realized their voices had grown louder.

After a brief pause, Yoshiaki explained in whispers how he'd dropped off some film at Shiba Photo that morning. He told her how access to the photos supplied info equivalent to peeping into their home and how the envelope had a space for the customer's phone number. He told her that the part-time delivery person was a man by the name of Hikuma.

"So that's it." Eriko was sobbing.

"Please, tell me, who on earth is this Hikuma?"

Eriko began haltingly. She spoke of an episode of bullying in junior high, something everyone experiences in one form or another. Some bullying victims turn to suicide, while others simply start skipping school. In Eriko's case, being bullied caused a psychological condition called hypochondria. *Hypochondria*... Yoshiaki had never thought of it as a diagnosis. Eriko told him her hypochondria had brought on temporary hearing loss.

In the second semester of freshman year in junior high, upon her father's death, Eriko had to transfer from a school in Yokohama to a public school in her mother's hometown in the countryside. A good student with a sharp sense of justice, she had earned the role of class representative at her Yokohama junior high, but after transferring, being unfamiliar with the new environment she kept a low profile. A handful of guys, the class bullies, picked on Eriko for being from a big city. She wasn't targeted for being unattractive; instead, the bullies were apparently incensed that she was a goodie-two-shoes with a conceited, urban style. Since she was tough, rather than grow timid she snapped back at the bullies, telling them to knock it off. This only served to aggravate them. If she'd simply held her mouth for just a while until the boys moved on to another target, her life might have turned out completely differently.

After that incident, the bullies escalated their attacks. Without reason, they would shove and poke her face and head, hide her belongings, trip her, and put chalk dust on her cafeteria lunch calling it "powdered cheese." Not a day would go by without them hurling abuse at her: *germ, ugly, fattie, die.*

"Wasn't there anyone to protect you?" Yoshiaki interrupted, unable to stand it any longer.

Eriko, still looking upwards, shook her head. Yoshiaki only heard the scraping against the pillow. "I had a few friends who were nice to me in the beginning, but afraid of the bullies, they all left me in the end."

"What about your teachers?"

"They told me to deal with it on my own."

Children's worlds are extremely narrow, and school is often their only social environment. How was she, ostracized and alone, supposed to deal with it?

Yoshiaki stretched an arm over his slumbering daughter's head and placed his hand on Eriko's shoulder, caressing her arm and giving it a strong squeeze.

She continued her story.

It was after the bullies spread a terrible rumor about Eriko that her body, particularly her sensory organs, chose to act up. All she had to do, as long as they were just poking her head, was endure the pain. After the rumor started, however, her feelings of alienation and humiliation reached the breaking point.

"Everyone says she got an abortion."

Her classmates were spreading the rumor. The number of her supposed pregnancies grew from one to two, then to three times, and soon she was labeled a whore who spread her legs for anyone. The originators of the rumor were no mystery. Suddenly, one day, her ear shunned the rumors.

Perhaps because the gang of bullies sat behind her on her right side, her right ear was the first one to go deaf. She had probably unconsciously tried to shut out any and all sounds from entering her ears. Being called things like "slut" and "whore" day in and day out shattered her pride, causing her hearing, and later even her vision, to fail.

"My ears would ring deep inside, and only the light drained out of everything I saw. It was like having a sheet of dark cellophane over my eyes…"

Yoshiaki recalled the only time he'd ever fainted, due to a bout of anemia, in the schoolyard of his elementary school. He still remembered the way light seemed to drain away during the split second before he fell. He thought it had to be a similar sensation as he tried to imagine Eriko's symptoms. For him, it had been momentary. As soon as the world seemed to change colors, he fainted, and after that was a blank. But for Eriko, the symptoms reoccurred over a prolonged period.

In the end, she could no longer attend school and spent each day holed up at home when she wasn't seeing a psychiatrist. Once the situation had reached that point, the school finally took action, calling the bullies into the principal's office for a thorough scolding. That, however, perversely served to incur the bullies' wrath. Soon they started calling her at home.

"You're just pretending you can't hear," they'd jeer.

Eriko never tried to go back to school.

The leader of the boys who had bullied Eriko and severely derailed her life was named Hikuma.

Puberty had probably rendered his voice unrecognizable to Eriko, which was why she hadn't realized the identity of the prank caller. Or maybe deep in her consciousness she did—hence the renewed signs of hypochondria and temporary loss of hearing.

When Yoshiaki proposed to Eriko four years ago, he was deeply shocked to learn that she only had a junior high education. He assumed there was some special reason since he knew her as a capable nutritionist with a job at a university hospital, but he never thought to needle her about the specifics. That mystery was now solved.

Even though Eriko refused to take any more classes, the junior high was considerate enough to grant her a diploma. Nonetheless, she gave up on the idea of getting into a high school and chose instead to attend a vocational school to become a nutritionist. As if to mend her wounded spirit, she hit the books hard and graduated with excellent grades. Yoshiaki and Eriko met when she was already working as a nutritionist at the hospital where he mistook her for a nurse during his stay after an accident.

His first impression of her was that she was smart. She had read a fair number of novels that were generally considered abstruse and got along well with Yoshiaki who'd graduated from a private university with a degree in literature. They shared similar tastes in music and movies, and he couldn't seem to get enough of her. The only thing that bothered him was her tendency to withdraw into herself at certain moments and the fact that she stubbornly refused to open up in a real way. Now the extent of the darkness she carried inside her heart had been laid bare.

Although she couldn't weep out loud with the baby right beside her, she continued to let out sobs. Her humiliation in junior high had come rushing back, and what she'd held in check deep inside her heart was pouring out like water from a broken dam.

Stroking her shoulder, Yoshiaki allowed the flood to run its course. "I'm taking the day off tomorrow."

Eriko simply responded with nods and didn't venture to ask her husband why.

10

Nearly four hours had passed since 9 a.m. when Yoshiaki started observing Hikuma. During those four hours, Yoshiaki had followed him at a reasonable distance and observed every detail he could. He felt as if he were peering into the life Hikuma had led up to then. The balance of information had been totally upset, giving Yoshiaki the advantage, which delighted him. At this point he could even identify a habit Hikuma had when he smoked.

Yoshiaki's initial plan was to wait for Hikuma at Shiba Photo at nine that morning, listen to him speak a few words to Kodama, and confirm that he was indeed the prank caller. Surprisingly, though, Hikuma hadn't said a word while he was at the shop. While Yoshiaki pretended to look for a disposable camera with his back to Hikuma, Kodama and the part-timer wordlessly exchanged the envelopes of film. After Hikuma stuffed them into a shoulder bag and left the store, Yoshiaki hastily followed him. He bought the same ticket as Hikuma at the subway station, and when transferring from the Toei Line to the Tozai Line, Yoshiaki was cautious enough to board the next car over, keeping an eye on Hikuma's profile from across the connector. He'd come all the way to Nishi Funabashi where the processing center was located. He was finding his unplanned turn as private eye downright exhilarating. While Hikuma wasn't likely to recognize his face just from the photos, staying out of his mark's direct line of sight was thrilling.

After getting off at Nishi Funabashi station, Hikuma slung his bag across his bony shoulder and started off on the ten-minute walk to the processing center. The bag held several dozen rolls of films he'd collected from photo shops around Shiba. Perhaps due to his sloping shoulders, Hikuma kept shifting the bag between his left and right sides. He looked thin and scrawny from behind. Since he'd been Eriko's classmate, he had to be twenty-nine. He was nearly as tall as Yoshiaki, but his arms and legs were extremely skinny and his shoulders were very narrow. He held himself ramrod straight and had a peculiar way of walking, taking short strides and dragging his feet. He wore a white short-sleeved shirt with vertical stripes and a pair of beige khakis. He had long hair and darkish skin and didn't wear glasses.

The six hours between the drop-off and pick-up at the processing center was free time. Hikuma walked back towards the station and killed over an hour at a pachinko parlor. He probably didn't have much money to play with;

once he realized the machines he'd chosen were a total bust, he stood diagonally behind one that was on a roll and glared stickily at the back of the customer working it. Standing at the entrance and watching Hikuma's profile, Yoshiaki tried to imagine what was going through the man's mind. *The machines I chose were no good, but the guy right in front of me has filled two large boxes already...* Was staring at such a sight an expression of mere envy, or was he trying to glean clues for winning by observing the path of the silver balls? The latter didn't seem to be the case as Hikuma's stare was concentrated on the back and hands of the fortunate customer.

It was ten minutes to one. It had been four hours since a whim had set Yoshiaki on this chase. Hikuma bought a racing newspaper from a kiosk and was slurping soba at a noodle stall in the station. Yoshiaki stood in the shadow of the kiosk and pretended to read a newspaper, glancing occasionally at Hikuma's back.

With the racing newspaper tucked under his arm, Hikuma exited the noodle stall. Perusing the folded paper, he retrieved a pack of cigarettes from his pocket and lit one with a lighter. He'd already smoked over ten cigarettes since that morning. Judging by his current pace, he smoked two or three packs a day.

He held the newspaper close to his face with his left hand and dangled the cigarette from his right as he walked through the sparse crowd in front of the bay of ticket machines. He walked with his eyes on the paper, not paying any attention to where he was going. Sometimes he lifted the cigarette to his mouth, exhaled smoke, and lowered his hand again, all the while approaching the kiosk where Yoshiaki was hiding.

In between them, a woman had stopped pushing her stroller and was retrieving her wallet from her purse. She left the stroller, in which a child of about two was dozing off, and walked towards the ticket machines. It happened right as she was feeding coins to a machine to buy a ticket. As Hikuma walked past, not bothering to look where he was going, his right hand brushed the face of the child in the stroller. The child started to cry all of a sudden as if he'd caught fire, which in a sense he had. In response, Hikuma's body jolted and he jumped to the side. The mother paused, coins still in hand, and turned towards her child. She hadn't been watching when the cherry of Hikuma's cigarette had pressed against the child's cheek. Hikuma seemed to realize that his cigarette had touched something soft. Glancing alternately between his cigarette and the child's screaming face, he fled the scene in a hurry. The mother crouched at the side of the child, whose face was bright red from crying, desperately trying to take the child's hand off its cheek. When she did, she saw ashes on the child's cheek. She looked all around her in confusion, still not comprehending what had happened to her child. In a dither, she could do nothing but look to the pedestrians around her with questioning eyes. Her face closely resembling the child's, she looked as though she was about to start crying herself.

At that point, Hikuma was turning the corner of the kiosk, and Yoshiaki unexpectedly got the chance to see his face up close. Hikuma was biting back a fit of laughter. Yoshiaki didn't miss Hikuma trying to hide his puffed cheeks with the newspaper and letting out short bursts of air. The man's face, which had worn a sullen, moody expression since that morning, was now giddily slack. Had the woman's distress been amusing to him? Or did he relish the sensation of his cigarette pressing into a child's cheek?

As Hikuma fled running from the scene, Yoshiaki turned and started to pursue him. Hardly checking for traffic, Hikuma darted across the street, flailed his arms as he tripped on a bump, and plunged into a park. Yoshiaki walked toward the park as well. Yet, no matter how far he walked, he couldn't shake off the child's wails. Even an outbound train thundering into the station couldn't block out the crying. A baby's protests were fiercer yet than the chorus of cicadas that would soon be filling the air. Yoshiaki thought of his daughter's soft cheeks.

After a brief nap in the park, Hikuma returned to the processing center and didn't come out for a full hour. He was probably sitting in some waiting area until the photos were ready. Yoshiaki, from his standby spot in the shadow of a fence, saw Hikuma coming out with a plump shoulder bag shortly after 4:00 p.m. He tailed him at a distance of about fifty yards. He wasn't worried about losing his mark since he knew Hikuma was heading for the station.

The cars of the inbound train originating from Nishi Funabashi were all fairly empty. Boarding the fourth one from the front, Hikuma flumped into a seat and stretched his legs out. As he had on the way out, Yoshiaki sat near the end of the next car over, positioning himself where he could observe Hikuma through the window.

The car was only about a quarter full so there was little danger of another passenger blocking his view. A few minutes after the train pulled away, Hikuma abruptly stood up and retrieved his shoulder bag from the baggage rack and put it on his lap. Yoshiaki bent forward, his hips nearly off the seat, to get his face closer to the window. Hikuma opened his shoulder bag's zipper, took out a bundle of envelopes, and pulled off the rubber band around them. He proceeded to remove the newly developed photos from their envelopes and to stare intently at each one. Yoshiaki pulled himself up to standing and looked down at Hikuma at an angle, his cheek right up against the window. Hikuma was far too absorbed in the photos to notice his presence on the other side of the glass.

Even though Yoshiaki had tailed him since that morning, he still hadn't gotten a single chance to hear the man speak. Excepting any exchanges inside the processing center, as far as Yoshiaki could tell, the man didn't utter a word to anyone. But there was no longer a need for him to speak—Yoshiaki was witnessing the proof of his theory.

Hikuma brought the photos to eye level and examined each as if glaring at them. When he was done with one envelope, he went on to the next, apparently planning to spend the whole half-hour until the transfer appreciating photography. Yoshiaki felt a chill run up his spine. Hikuma had been looking at other people's photos ever since starting at the job in the beginning of February. One day, he'd discovered Eriko's face in there by coincidence. The girl he'd tormented endlessly in junior high… Maybe at first he thought she was someone else who bore a resemblance. Fifteen years could alter one's face significantly. But something rang a bell in his mind. As bully and victim, they had been no strangers. Next, he realized that there was a way to determine if it was indeed Eriko. He copied down the customer's number written on the envelope and tried it when he got home. Upon hearing her voice, he grew certain. No mistake, it was Eriko. The victim he'd driven to tears and whose life he'd managed to derail.

The pictures no doubt featured different compositions and people, but Hikuma continued to probe them with the same lifeless gaze. Yoshiaki tried to surmise what this man might have felt. Upon seeing the girl he'd tormented to hell all grown up, what ripples had disturbed his heart?

The film Yoshiaki had had developed in early February were of a trip to hot spring resorts over the end of last year and into the new year. They'd spent four days staying at various B&Bs in Izu and visiting hot springs. The camera set on auto, Yoshiaki had his arms wrapped protectively about his heavily pregnant wife's shoulders. From the photos, Eriko must have appeared unabashedly, innocently happy.

The film dropped off after the May holidays must have fanned Hikuma's jealousy even more. A brand new home, the happy expression of an expecting mother, delivery, child-rearing... Eriko's big task, all condensed into thirty-six photos. His former victim's happy face and lifestyle had unfolded like a tapestry before his eyes. Comparing their respective circumstances, it would have been obvious that their positions had switched. The person he once beat down, made cry, and verbally abused now stood on a higher level and could look down on him. Doubtlessly, he couldn't bear it. How kind of them to leave their new phone number right there on the envelope. Calling them at their new home was in fact all too easy, a no-brainer, for Hikuma.

Perhaps due to having observed him since nine in the morning, Yoshiaki could almost hear Hikuma's thoughts. Having seen how the man had spent the day, Yoshiaki could well imagine what kind of life Hikuma had led up until now. He had to be a weak person. Hikuma likely had no idea just how hard Eriko had struggled to patch up the yawning darkness that had opened inside her and to complete her training as a nutritionist when she'd never even really finished junior high. Instead of dragging others down to her level, she'd crawled up, embarking on a new path to overcome that darkness. Failing to picture that process and merely raging with jealousy in face of the result... Watching Hikuma, what Yoshiaki felt was less hatred than enervation. Just looking at the man threatened to diminish his own desire to face life.

The Tozai subway train passed across Urayasu Bridge on its way into Tokyo. Noticing the altered sound of the rails, Hikuma looked up briefly from the photos and checked his wristwatch. He was probably estimating the time until his transfer at Nihonbashi. He gazed upward for a while, then shook his head back and forth and retrieved the next photo from the envelope.

The train sank underground right before Minami Sunamachi station. Nearly every seat in the car was taken. With passengers standing in between them, Yoshiaki didn't have a clear view of Hikuma without shifting. One stop before Nihonbashi, perhaps having finished looking at all the photos, Hikuma returned the bundle of envelopes to his shoulder bag and stood up. He leaned on a door and started rapping at the glass with his fist. Hikuma continued to punch the same spot with his lightly balled fist until he transferred.

11

A light in one apartment switched on within the gloom. The dim, vague illumination spilled from a wood-framed window on the rear of the second floor and seeped onto the downtown alleyway below. After a quick glance around, Yoshiaki confirmed that the only other light came from a room on the north side of the first floor. Hikuma had just now returned to his apartment after getting off work, walked through the entrance, and disappeared into the second floor. Following him with his eyes, Yoshiaki looked up at the apartment and made a note of its location. He then went around to the front entrance and copied down the address.

"Ota Ward, Haneda 7th Street... Okada Lodgings."

Now that he had the address, the guy couldn't escape. As Yoshiaki sighed with relief, he realized he was hungry. Too engrossed in tracking Hikuma, he hadn't had anything to eat since nibbling at a sandwich a little before nine. Mentally retracing the route from Anamori-Inari station to where he stood now, he tried to remember if there'd been a suitable eatery. He recalled seeing a Chinese place right around the corner. He turned his back on the apartment building and walked several paces. His stride, however, began to shorten, and he soon came to a halt.

I'm trying to run away.

Yoshiaki realized that he was using hunger as an excuse to postpone a confrontation with Hikuma and to procrastinate

140

at some Chinese restaurant. Not doing what he needed to do at the right moment could lead to never finishing this at all.

Under normal circumstances, Yoshiaki rarely missed a chance to act. He was blessed with enough dynamism to put his thoughts into action straight away. But after following Hikuma for over ten hours, he was flattened. It was as though Hikuma's back emitted a powerful aura that negated people's energy and willpower.

Yoshiaki took a deep breath and walked into the apartment building.

Shoes had to be removed at the entrance, forcing residents and visitors to make their way upstairs barefoot in a setup akin to a boarding house. The steep stairwell squeaked as Yoshiaki climbed up, gripping the railing as he went. There were four rooms on each side of a hallway lined with a stained, dark-red carpet. The farthest room on the right had to be Hikuma's. Yoshiaki stood before it and pressed an ear against the sliding door to discern what was happening inside. He heard a voice. It wasn't a conversation but a one-sided harangue. Was he making another prank call? Yoshiaki listened intently. Even through the door, he could confirm that it was the same voice as the prank caller's.

Fragments of speech reached Yoshiaki's ear.

"...moron.... shit doesn't work... carin' for that brat... listen... I'll make you cry... Put you and your kid underwater and... a pool.... Who was the one who bawled..."

He was calling Yoshiaki's home. Realizing that right now, at this very moment, his wife was at home listening to this voice and trembling violently, Yoshiaki let his rage get the better of him and flung the door open with all his might. As it was unlocked, it slid freely along the track and slammed into the wooden frame with a bang.

Hikuma, who was lying sprawled out with the receiver tucked between his ear and shoulder, sprang into sitting as the words died in his throat. Yoshiaki stepped inside the apartment and pressed the record button on the tape recorder hidden inside his jacket pocket.

"Who were you calling?" Yoshiaki asked before Hikuma could speak.

Eyes wide open, Hikuma flapped his mouth briefly before voicing a quiet "Oh."

"Seems you've figured out who I am." Yoshiaki closed the door behind him and stood blocking the way.

The lone ten-watt fluorescent bulb above the sink did little to brighten the four-and-a-half-tatami space saturated with cigarette smoke. An empty socket dangled from a lamp cord hanging from the center of the ceiling. Outside, Yoshiaki had spotted the same weak beam given off by the ten-watt florescent bulb above the sink. He glanced around briefly but didn't note any other source of light. It seemed very much like Hikuma to live under dim fluorescent lighting. The man embraced darkness, and not just inside him.

Looking cowed, Hikuma returned the receiver to the hook.

"Who were you calling?" Yoshiaki repeated.

"How dare you barge in," Hikuma pouted.

"You son of a bitch. You're the bastard who barged in over the phone!"

Falling silent, Hikuma looked searchingly at Yoshiaki, who still blocked the doorway. The prank caller was sizing up his opponent. Confronted by a clearly hostile man in a small room, the first thing you needed to do was gauge your relative physical prowess. In Hikuma's case, it didn't take long for realization to set in. He had no chance of coming out on top against Yoshiaki in a tussle, so he turned his face away, leaned against the wall, and hugged his knees.

Then he gave an unctuous smirk. "Thought you looked familiar. Weren't you around Nishifuna today?"

He probably remembered seeing Yoshiaki once or twice. Without deigning to answer, Yoshiaki knelt on the edge of the carpet, pulled the phone over, and pressed redial to confirm the number Hikuma had been calling.

The phone beeped out the sequence. The call connected, rang five times, and a machine picked up. Yoshiaki heard his own voice: "Hello, this is the Fukazawa residence. We cannot take your call right now..."

Yoshiaki pushed down the hook to disconnect the call. "Why do you do this?" he asked.

Hikuma, still avoiding eye contact, drew his lighter closer. His temple quivered as he lit a cigarette. Yoshiaki, who had been glaring wordlessly at Hikuma, surveyed the room in an effort to calm down.

It was a dingy place with no private bath or toilet. This had to be the best Hikuma could afford on the less than hundred thou a month his part-time job brought in. The only luxury in his apartment was the touchtone phone, which sat directly on the carpet, the coiled cord tossed into a corner against the wall. Everything had a sense of imbalance. A few t-shirts, briefs, and socks were hung up to dry on a clothesline by the window, underneath which was a cheap metal bed frame. As Yoshiaki's gaze continued further down, he noted that the beige carpet was covered in countless burn marks that looked like creeping caterpillars. As the burns were concentrated around the bed, it was clear that they were caused by Hikuma smoking in bed. Some marks had burned so deep they went through the carpet to the tatami matting underneath. Below the kitchen sink were empty bottles of *shochu* gin and beer cans.

Cigarettes, alcohol, and prank calls, Yoshiaki thought to himself.

Hikuma, eyes narrowed, took shallow, fidgety drags off his cigarette. He gripped the lighter in his right hand and seemed determined to avoid eye contact.

The man started to get on Yoshiaki's nerves to an unspeakable degree. He wanted to punch the guy in the face until he vomited blood. The urge was transmitted from his chest, to his arm, to the tips of his fingers.

"Say something, dammit!"

He struck the wall with his fist, causing the cups in the sink to rattle.

"Say something, like what?"

The lazy vowels, followed by a sloppy grin. Hikuma repeatedly sparked and clicked off his lighter. If he'd had a knife, he'd no doubt have flashed it. The lighter was standing in for one. Hikuma probably didn't realize himself that he was drawing on the power of fire to try to intimidate his adversary.

"Why did you prank call Eriko?" Yoshiaki bit out.

"No reason." Hikuma's smirk didn't fade.

"Knock that idiotic smile off your face," Yoshiaki growled menacingly.

He could hear a gulp as Hikuma swallowed. "I called 'cause I wanted to. That's all."

"So you're admitting to placing those prank calls."

Hikuma, cigarette in mouth, garbled, "The hell you saying?" His cigarette dropped to the carpet, leaving a new burn.

"Please, I'm asking you to stop calling us."

In response to Yoshiaki's shift in tone, Hikuma relented a little. "Dunno. I can't promise anything."

"I need you to."

Hikuma laughed out loud. "What happens if I don't?"

"We've already reported your calls to the police. All I have to do next is tell them I've identified the culprit and produce this tape."

Yoshiaki took out the small recorder from his pocket.

"I've been taping this conversation. It's clear that you're the caller."

"I never said I made those calls."

"You fucking idiot. Did you forget that we have an answering machine? Your voice is recorded on it. Anyone could tell it's the same voice."

Hikuma's eyes turned grim as he sparked his lighter with increasing frequency. Where previously he'd kept his gaze averted, he now stared tenaciously at Yoshiaki. He looked peeved, seemingly lost in thought, but then suddenly his face went slack. The persistence of the guy's smirk was unsettling to Yoshiaki.

"Do not call us again, got it? Or I'll report you to the police," Yoshiaki repeated for emphasis, tucked the recorder back into his pocket, and got to his feet. The tape was still recording. He didn't want to stay in the room any longer. It wasn't just the gloom or the smell—something about the room made it intolerable.

When Yoshiaki made to open the sliding door, suddenly that drawling, viscous voice uttered, "Hey, maybe I should just toss your brat out the window, like a ball, ah?"

Hand still on the door, Yoshiaki didn't even turn around. Shaken, he must have stood there for a good ten seconds. Yet, during those moments, the menace Hikuma's words portended played in its entirety across his mind's eye.

Indeed, even if he were to turn Hikuma in to the police, they wouldn't throw him in jail just for prank calls. He'd probably get a thorough scolding, but that would be it. Yoshiaki was well aware that Hikuma was one to hold a grudge. If he resented Yoshiaki's actions there was no telling what he might do. He might even throw their baby out the window just as he'd said. He thought he could hear his wife's tearful screaming. There were many ways to get her to open the front door while her husband wasn't home. Hikuma would wrestle with his wife, race down the hall, grab the sleeping baby, tuck her under his arm… His wife begging for mercy… Such scenes pulsated in Yoshiaki's mind; at the same time, rage surged through him. It may have been an empty threat, but as long as Hikuma lived, Yoshiaki and his family would have to live in fear. He knew the man didn't mean it. He knew that placing prank calls was the most Hikuma could do, that he wasn't the type to actually take drastic measures. But there was always a tiny chance… Every day during the week from 7:00 a.m. to 9:00 p.m., Yoshiaki wasn't at home. At work, even that slight chance would rob him of all focus. Was there no way to remove the danger once and for all?

There was—just one way. He couldn't allow his wife and his daughter to remain unprotected. Eriko was no longer struggling alone and unassisted.

In his thirty-one years of life, Yoshiaki had never experienced such righteous rage. If he could just snap this bastard's neck, he wouldn't need to worry anymore. If he left him alone, his family would have to live in fear indeterminately.

Yoshiaki stuck his hand in his pocket and switched off the tape recorder. Slowly, he turned back around. "I couldn't quite hear you... Care to repeat that?"

His demeanor had undergone a shocking change. Hikuma's cigarette slipped from his mouth again.

12

When Eriko opened the blinds, the autumnal sun filtered into the room. Yoshiaki covered his forehead with his hand and moaned, but it was far more refreshing to be woken by natural light than the electronic sounds of an alarm clock.

"C'mon, up and at 'em. You promised." Eriko was looking much younger than usual in her sweatshirt and jeans, and her movements were brisk.

"What time is it?" Yoshiaki asked.

"It's nine o'clock. You've slept enough, haven't you?"

"Nine..."

He had slept for more than ten hours, almost twice as long as usual.

Yoshiaki hadn't forgotten about the promise he made to Eriko the night before. He'd gone into the office to catch up on some work though it was a Saturday. As soon as he'd returned, Eriko had asked him to take her out somewhere the next day. "All right. Let's go to Kamakura," he'd replied before falling asleep. Lured by the clear autumn skies, he did feel like visiting a number of temples in Kamakura he hadn't seen in a while.

Still in his pajamas, he walked towards the bathroom. He glanced towards the entrance and noticed a daypack by the door. Surprisingly enough, his wife was already prepared—just how early had she risen? While sighing at her meticulousness, he found it endearing that Eriko would be so excited over a day trip to Kamakura. Being housebound for long thanks to childrearing apparently put you on cloud nine over a mere hike. Baby Aya was now six months old, and there wasn't anywhere they couldn't go so long as they had a stroller or sling. From now on there would be more opportunities for family trips.

Yoshiaki himself required just ten minutes to get ready as all he needed to do was shave and wash his face; he always ended up being the one trying to get Eriko out the door. Today was no different. While she was still hustling about looking for wetnaps for the baby, Yoshiaki already had his shoes on in the foyer. "Come on, let's get going," he hollered time and again.

Carrying the baby in the elevator hall he asked, "Newspaper?"

Eriko shook her head. "I haven't yet."

The papers weren't delivered to each individual apartment but were left in the communal mailbox in the lobby. Each tenant had to pick them up themselves, but Eriko hadn't gotten theirs yet this morning. Wanting to read it in the train, he retrieved theirs as they passed through the lobby and stuffed it into the daypack.

Transferring at Yokohama station from the Toyoko Line to the Yokosuka Line, they were able to sit as a family in box seating facing each other. Yoshiaki took out the morning edition dated October 16th and started reading it from the local news section as usual. Eriko chattered incessantly at him, but he was too busy scanning the headlines and answered vaguely. He wasn't searching for any article in particular. That Sunday morning edition featured a color photo of Mt. Bandai's foliage turning autumnal and the report of a famous politician's death. Neither item interested Yoshiaki. Instead, his eyes were drawn to the lower left corner of the local news section. He saw a curiously attention-grabbing name and address in the small print.

The headline stated that there had been a fire in Haneda, Ota Ward.

…Last night after 8:00 p.m. a fire broke out on the second floor of the Okada Lodgings apartment building in Haneda, Ota Ward…

Yoshiaki held his breath and brought the paper closer to his face.

… The burned corpse of Yuji Hikuma, age 29, a resident, was found among the ruins… The fire may have come from the victim's apartment on the second floor, but the cause is still undetermined…

Yoshiaki took a deep breath.

How the fire started?

It was obvious. Though it had been three and a half months ago, the scorch marks all over the carpet were still clearly burned into the back of his eyelids. That room had brimmed with a certain something that augured such a fate. After getting hammered, Hikuma had probably fallen asleep with a cigarette in his hand, and by the time he realized, there was no escaping the flames and he'd burned to death…

Three and a half months ago ...

Yoshiaki, infuriated by Hikuma's threat that he'd throw Aya out the window, turned around with murder in his eyes. Hikuma's cigarette fell out of his mouth. Before he could grab it, Yoshiaki snatched it up and grabbed Hikuma by the scruff of his neck.

"Go on. Try saying that one more time," Yoshiaki growled, but on Hikuma's face his smirk stayed plastered over an expression that was neither fear nor resignation. Yoshiaki's hand moved of its own volition. Instead of punching him, Yoshiaki pressed the cigarette's cherry into Hikuma's slackened cheek. Crying out like a child, the guy writhed. Yoshiaki bore down onto him, pinning him in place, and ground the cigarette into his face. The smell of burning flesh felt repugnant for a moment, but letting go wasn't an option. Yoshiaki had to make him understand, tangibly, that he was deadly serious. The paper of the cigarette broke and the leaves crumbled away until only the filter remained, but he didn't let up. Then, leaning in close enough to bite off Hikuma's earlobe, he drove his point home repeatedly: "If you ever call us again or loiter anywhere near our home, I'll smash every single bone in your body."

Hikuma started to moan and sob, his tears dripping onto the floor. He looked just like a baby when he cried. The strength in Yoshiaki's arms dissipated.

"Shit! Shi-Shit!"

Hikuma continued to weep, hand to his cheek. Yoshiaki had never seen a man cry with such unashamed abandon. His murderous urge to strangle Hikuma faded away like a dream. Thoughts of getting arrested for murder and his wife being left with the baby and the mortgage flitted through his mind, but more than anything it was Hikuma's moans that sapped his desire for violence.

Yoshiaki stood up and looked down at Hikuma, who kept on crying curled up in the fetal position, clawing at air. Sometimes he would pound his own knees with his fists, but rather than lash out at Yoshiaki, anger and protestations directed at something deeper seemed to be bubbling up in him. He scraped his legs against the carpet and contorted his face, sloppy from tears and drool. Gradually, he started to grumble. Since his speech was lazy to begin with the words were unintelligible, but it was clear he wasn't addressing Yoshiaki. Hikuma's face was turned elsewhere, and he griped endlessly, cursing and unleashing his wrath at whomever it was who hovered beyond the darkness. Yoshiaki thought Hikuma had lost his mind.

Three and a half months had passed since that indelible scene, and during that time there were no more prank calls, and Hikuma certainly hadn't been seen loitering around their neighborhood. Eriko had ceased to be afraid of the phone ringing. Yoshiaki was learning of Hikuma's demise just when the caller's shadow had finally retreated from the daily lives of the Fukazawas.

The Yokosuka train was about to roll into Higashi Totsuka station. Yoshiaki glanced out with his newspaper still open in front of him. As small groups of people waiting on the platform passed slowly by the window, he wondered, at this late point in time, what kind of life Hikuma had really led. Did his mother dote on him? What was his relationship like with his father? Did his parents have a healthy marriage? Did he have any siblings? What were his dreams when he moved to Tokyo from the provinces? What work had he done before delivering film? Had he ever loved a woman? How many times in his life had he truly felt that life was wonderful? It was impossible to know now.

The newspaper spread out in front of his face grew two bumps in the center. His daughter, sitting on her mother's lap, was kicking at it. *Daddy, Daddy...* It was like a voiceless call, and he shifted the paper to the side to see her face.

"What's wrong, honey?" Eriko squinted her nearsighted eyes and hunched over, peering into his face.

"Oh, nothing." Yoshiaki wiped at his eyes in a fluster and put the newspaper on the overhead rack.

"Some sad article?"

"No, not really..."

He had no intention of telling Eriko about the death. Yoshiaki wanted her to be able to put this behind her without any mention of it.

His hands now empty, Yoshiaki took his daughter on his lap and spoke to her in baby talk, but tears continued to spill from his eyes. He didn't know why he was crying. Certainly, Hikuma's death had brought him a measure of relief. Although his threats to Hikuma had effectively halted the prank calls for the last three and a half months, the guy's shadow had always lurked in the back of his mind. With Hikuma dead, Yoshiaki was free at last. That loathsome voice would never come back to haunt them. What was odd was that Yoshiaki could forgive Hikuma while still detesting him. It wasn't pity or a sense of superiority over their respective circumstances. Perhaps it was his daughter's innocent smile, but somehow all of humanity including Hikuma and himself seemed endearing to Yoshiaki.

Looking around the interior of the carriage he saw a

good number of families, probably out to enjoy the clear, autumnal Sunday. Happiness didn't take a more hackneyed form than this. A family's respite rested on understanding that somewhere out there people like Hikuma haunted the shadows waiting for an opportune moment. The thought briefly crossed Yoshiaki's mind as the train rocked into motion.

Embrace

Rieko turned off the shower, thinking she heard the phone ringing, and listened intently. She opened the bathroom door and poked her head through the narrow crack but heard nothing from the direction of the living room where the phone was. *Must have been my imagination.* The steam from the shower that filled the small space handily amplified any sound that reached her ears.

Her daughter, who had turned one in January, was crawling along the styrofoam mat on the bathroom floor and making squeaky, obnoxious noises. Rieko removed Kiko's hearing aid before baths and before bed. Kiko, born with impaired hearing, couldn't register any external sounds without such a device. Even when water gushed out of the faucet, Kiko's mind was wrapped in silence.

Rieko finished rinsing out her own hair and wrapped her head with a towel. Still half-damp herself, she meticulously dried off her daughter's body. Whenever Rieko bathed or dried her daughter, she made it a habit to place a hand behind the neck even though Kiko was at a stage where she could support her own head. The baby was maintaining a healthy weight. Rieko couldn't help but think her neck was fragile.

The gas-powered space heater burning bright red made the living room feel overly warm to her post-shower skin. As she had to bathe both herself and her daughter, it tended to take a long time, and even during this, the coldest season of the year, she was sweating by the time she came out of the bathroom.

While she dressed her daughter in pajamas, Rieko glanced at the clock. The needles were lining up to nine. As Rieko knelt naked on the floor with both hands on the floor, Kiko kicked up a foot and struck one of her breasts. Just then the phone rang. It was 9:00 on the dot, as promised.

As anticipated, it was Fujimura. He must have been calling from a payphone along a road somewhere. She could hear the muffled sound of cars whizzing by and splashing up rainwater in the background. Rieko's new house on the outskirts of the city of Shimizu was a new building with aluminum sashes and shutters protecting the windows, preventing outside noise from seeping in, so she would often be oblivious to precipitation. She could now sense the frigid sounds of the end of February through the phone. The noises that night were dripping wet. The receiver was acting like a hearing aid, amplifying all sorts of sounds.

"Can you guess where I am now?"

Whenever someone asked such a question, it meant they were somewhere the listener would never imagine.

"I guess it's someplace rainy."

Tokyo, where Fujimura lived, and Shimizu were close to a hundred miles apart. Perhaps it was coming down hard in both cities, but Rieko sensed rain outside her own shutters. She was convinced that Fujimura must be near her house.

At the unexpected answer, Fujimura made a choked noise, at a loss for how to respond. He seemed to fear that he wasn't welcome.

"So you must be nearby?" Rieko added hurriedly.

"Oh, you can tell?"

"Sure can."

"And you're not surprised?"

"I thought you were drunk and it was some joke…"

Fujimura fell silent. He was apparently waiting for Rieko's invitation.

"So what are your plans for the rest of the evening?" she asked, somewhat appalled.

"Well, I dunno…" Fujimura said, then laughed as if to conceal his discomfort.

"Would you like to come over to my humble abode?" Rieko noticed that one of Kiko's pajama buttons was undone. She tucked the receiver between her ear and shoulder and dexterously fixed it.

"I would appreciate that," Fujimura replied, sounding genuinely relieved. "I was wondering what I'd do if you didn't let me in after coming all this way from Tokyo."

Did you really drive all the way out here just to see me?

Rieko doubted his words. Common sense argued against such a thing. Fujimura, who worked in sales and traveled often, probably had come just a little out of his way in order to see her.

"Liar. You just dropped by because you're on a business trip and you came just a little out of your way to see me," Rieko said out loud to taunt him.

"Oh, stop. It's Saturday. I'm off work," Fujimura insisted desperately. *I raced along the Tomei Expressway in the rain just to see you, that's the only reason, I swear.*

"What were you planning to do if I wasn't home?"

"I took a gamble on that point."

The intensity of the male sex drive always astonished Rieko. At the same time, she was stunned by Fujimura's cavalier attitude given the length of the round-trip journey. Yet she thought it a little unfair that he waited to call until he was nearby. She was flattered that he'd come all this way, and thinking of the distance he'd driven she wasn't ready to flatly refuse him and send him home. Despite a good chance that he'd end up wasting his time, he'd spared no effort at the hint of an opportunity. As a woman, it was something Rieko could hardly even imagine doing. The only thing she unreservedly put all her energy into these days was her daughter.

Rieko and Fujimura had met five nights ago through work.

As the owner of a boutique on main street in Shimizu, Rieko had a business meeting with a major apparel manufacturer. Fujimura was the manufacturer's sales rep. During a pause in their discussions, Fujimura had asked her out for a drink. He apparently concluded from the casual chatter woven through their otherwise business-focused exchanges that Rieko could hold her liquor. He invited her with an air of confidence.

Fujimura was tall and slim with a slender but fearless face, which suited Rieko's tastes. She had doubted that he'd be able to return to Tokyo that night if he went out drinking in Shimizu. Nevertheless, she'd vaguely replied, "I guess…"

with a coy tilt of her head and gone to ring her mother. If she couldn't watch Kiko, Rieko couldn't possibly spend a night out. Her mother agreed to babysit on the condition that Kiko would be asleep by the time she got there.

Rieko was upbeat over the prospect of her first night out in a while. Her impatience must have seeped across her skin; Kiko, who always slept beside her, took a long time to doze off. It was nearly ten by the time she met up with Fujimura at the tiny bar. It was no longer possible for him to make the last bullet train back to Tokyo. As Fujimura waded deeper into intoxication, his ulterior motive began to surface. Around when alcohol started to dissolve reason he offered, "I booked a hotel room for the night. Why don't we continue drinking there?"

Rieko wasn't interested. She realized that she had probably led him on and tried to let him down easily. Emboldened by her inebriation, she ended up speaking in a blunt manner that only served to incite male curiosity.

"No way. I've got small tits and a chubby tummy. I can't possibly get naked in front of a man."

Fujimura laughed. He was amused that an invitation for a drink in a hotel room had been rejected on the basis of physical flaws.

"You don't look that way to me at all." His eyes, as he took in Rieko's figure, filled with irrepressible desire. Having one's mind read by others is discomfiting for a man or woman, but even Fujimura was aware of how comically obvious he was, gazing at her body after making such a remark. Still, he didn't bother to look away. In fact, he believed a woman had to have some confidence in her appearance to be self-deprecating. He suspected just the opposite of what she said. At thirty-two, she was just starting to bloom with a ripe loveliness.

Of course, the real reason Rieko didn't want to sleep with Fujimura lay elsewhere. She didn't have the heart to abandon her deaf daughter for the sake of soaking in pleasure. Her divorce had just been finalized at the beginning of that month, and including the time she was separated from her husband, she hadn't been locked in an embrace with a man for almost a year. Some of her friends advised her to have fun once in a while simply to shake things up, but she couldn't seem to take the first step. Pent-up sexual frustration, she knew, wouldn't help with her childrearing, but she hadn't wanted to be intimate with a man for a while.

"Maybe next time. I ought to go home tonight." Rieko glanced at her watch and made to stand up. Her daughter's sleeping face had suddenly popped into her head. She thought she heard a faint cry.

"Then when can I see you again?" Fujimura asked, oddly formal, readily retreating. Since she'd said "next time" he must have decided there was hope down along the line.

"Well…"

Rieko was still trying to decide what to say to him when he spoke as if the thought had just struck him. "I'll call you at exactly nine p.m. this Saturday."

Rieko had casually mentioned that only on Saturdays, rather than staying at her mother's home, she spent the night with her daughter at her large new house on the outskirts they'd purchased upon the baby's arrival.

"You'd feel safe with Kiko there, right?"

What do you mean, "feel safe"? Did it mean he wouldn't attempt to pull any funny stuff in front of her child? Or that

162

as a mother she'd feel safer with her daughter beside her?

The majority of men who wooed her saying they'd been waiting for her to get divorced quite indifferently invited her to bed, and when rejected, backed off as quickly as they'd approached. They all had it wrong. They seemed to think that the body of a woman newly freed from marital life was brimming with desire and that she would indiscriminately bed anyone who crossed her path. How shallow. Rieko was confident that even if men shunned her completely from here on out she wouldn't feel all that inconvenienced.

Fujimura didn't seem stupid enough to think that the male and female sex drives were the same. She appreciated how graciously he'd backed off when denied, and something about him made her sense that he understood her maternal feelings toward her daughter. She had never felt that way talking to other men. So when Fujimura said he'd call at nine on Saturday, Rieko indicated that she was looking forward to it. She believed that as long as it was someone she could readily communicate with, she wouldn't get trapped in a quagmire.

After giving Fujimura turn-by-turn directions to her home, she hung up, reapplied a touch of makeup, picked up the clutter in the living room, and used the vacuum she hadn't touched in weeks. As she only stayed in the new house on Saturdays, she rarely vacuumed the place. The house with its three Western-style rooms in addition to two interconnected tatami rooms, plus a 300-square-foot living room, was too large for just her and daughter. Two years ago, she'd had an architect acquaintance design it on the assumption that she was going to have at least two kids. In an ironic twist, her relationship with her husband had turned frosty by the time the house was finished, and after only two months in their new home, her husband moved out. The land was in Rieko's mother's name and Rieko had paid the lion's share of the construction costs, so it was only natural for her ex-husband to be the one to move out. Since then, as she couldn't very well leave a young daughter behind while running about for work, they primarily lived at her mother's home, only returning to the new house once a week to let the air circulate. Her mother, who lived alone, stubbornly refused to leave the house she was used to, so there was no choice but for Rieko to crawl back to her mother's place.

Rieko decided she would let the evening take its course. Her daughter was where she could constantly keep an eye on her, sleeping peacefully, her hearing aid removed. Even though Kiko sensed things, sounds would never wake her.

Opening the door almost as soon as the doorbell rang, Rieko found Fujimura standing there with a beautifully wrapped gift tucked under his arm. His hair and the shoulders of his sweater were wet and he was obviously freezing. She showed him to the living room and offered him a seat on the sofa.

"How's Kiko?" he asked as he sat down.

Was he really concerned about her deaf daughter? Or was he just trying to confirm the location of the nuisance? His true intent was unclear to Rieko. His asking about her daughter, however, did make her happy. Rieko was sure that Kiko was why she and her husband had divorced. When people asked about the separation, though, she cited her ex's gambling problem as the reason.

She had only learned of her husband's vice six months ago. He'd started spending longer and longer away from home without notice, and his blatant lies were becoming more obvious. At first she thought he was having an affair, but after some questioning, he confessed he was hooked on auto-bike and motorboat racing. As Rieko sighed with relief and appeared to lose interest, her husband cast his eyes downward and confessed he owed money to loan sharks.

"How much?"

"About 2.5 million yen…"

It was an amount he couldn't repay without her help, he said, and he'd been waiting for the right time to consult with her.

"Tell me the truth, from the beginning," she demanded harshly, expressing disbelief at her husband's irresponsibility when their daughter's care was costing them a small fortune. Apparently he had owed 500,000 yen around the time they got married and been paying back 50,000 yen each month. He found himself incapable of quitting, and over the last three years, his debt had neither increased nor decreased. During that stretch he was somehow managing with his own pocket money, so it was not unforgivable. Yet after a certain period, his spending on gambling suddenly shot up, the stable debt becoming a thing of the past last January. Essentially, his gambling worsened around the time of Kiko's birth. That alone was something Rieko simply could not forgive.

Shouldn't it be the opposite? You're supposed to stop gambling once you have a child, Rieko shouted in her heart. *Especially with her hearing problem…* His lack of love for his baby, or rather, his resentment at the child being born at all was there boldly laid out in numbers. It was like taking a peek into the depths of her husband's heart. She felt badly betrayed. If the debt had stayed level, the marriage might have lasted, but her husband had never once bought anything for their daughter and sunk large sums into gambling.

"This is for Kiko," Fujimura said, handing Rieko the gift wrapped in lovely floral paper. Rieko made a dramatic expression of surprise and bowed in gratitude, then immediately opened the present. Inside were pajamas with the same floral pattern as the wrapping paper. A rapidly growing infant could always use more pajamas.

"They're adorable!" Rieko practically screamed and gave him a huge smile. In place of thanks, she asked, "How about a whiskey and water?"

"Please. Sorry, I feel like I've intruded," replied Fujimura, all of a sudden oddly formal, his voice lowered so as not to wake Kiko.

"It's okay. She's already asleep. Besides…"

"Oh, right." Fujimura ducked his head awkwardly and, seemingly at a loss, glanced around the room. He looked so pitiably stiff and nervous that a drink to loosen him up certainly seemed in order.

Rieko mixed a double whiskey with water and handed it to him.

Even under the living room's unforgiving fluorescent light, Fujimura did not look like a 35-year-old man with a wife and a young child. He'd said he'd only pitched up to high school, but his body was still firm with no excess fat, and his artless nature coupled with traces of boyishness in his features gave him a youthful appearance. He didn't seem to sport any affectations, and the way he backed off when he sensed tension was extremely reassuring. Otherwise, she would never have let a man she hardly knew into her home so late at night.

After an hour, Fujimura and Rieko had put away three glasses of whiskey and water each. Under the bright fluorescent light, Rieko's cheeks were tinted red, and her oval, lightly made-up face glowed.

During a lull in their conversation, he leaned in towards her and called her name in a sweet voice.

She looked away. She pictured in her mind's eye how the situation might unfold just a few seconds later—imagined that he would reach out and pull her to his chest. Part of her wanted to let things run their course, but she felt strangely cool and disengaged from herself. Perhaps she'd been waiting for this all day. She could deny it mentally, but the depths of her body seemed ready to accept him.

Yet that syrupy moment lasted only a second. Rieko was yanked back into reality by a forlorn cry like a cat meowing in the distance.

Kiko's hands wandered about in search of her mother, who should have been right at her side. Rieko sprang up and ran into the adjacent Japanese-style room. Fujimura, who had gone into a half-crouch, could only sit back down again.

Since Kiko refused to go back to sleep and Rieko didn't seem to be coming back to the living room anytime soon, Fujimura tried to listen through the sliding door. Even though Kiko couldn't hear, Rieko was nevertheless enthusiastically talking to her. Though the baby's cries grew louder as if in response, Fujimura didn't sense from them the signature vitality of a child's tantrum. He could tell how the communication between mother and daughter in the dark room on the other side of the sliding door relied on touch.

After about twenty minutes, Rieko finally reappeared. She didn't miss the look of disappointment that flashed across Fujimura's face as soon as she emerged. Kiko was tied to her back with a sling, the band of which dug into her modest cleavage.

"I'm sorry to come out like this. She just doesn't want to go back to sleep."

Fujimura gave a strained smile, took Kiko's hands in his, and said, "Good evening."

With her hands thus held, Kiko's face relaxed, and she smiled showing her small white teeth, belying her tears from just a moment ago. Rieko tilted her head to examine the shift in her daughter's expression.

"Oh? Weird. I thought you were supposed to be shy." She wasn't trying to flatter Fujimura. Kiko was almost guaranteed to burst into tears when confronted with a strange man.

"I've lost a daughter too," Fujimura said, still holding Kiko's hand.

Startled, Rieko narrowed her eyes at him. *What do you mean, "too"? I've never lost a child. Kiko's just deaf.*

Ignorant of Rieko's silent protest, Fujimura dropped his gaze to the carpet and began to talk about his daughter.

It happened when his daughter was a year-and-a-half old, the day after his wife, a nurse, had worked a night shift at the hospital. Since his wife went to sleep as soon as she got back from late-night stints at the general hospital, it fell to Fujimura to take his daughter to daycare. As usual, he took her on his bicycle and dropped her off.

"Okay, Yoko. Take care." He pat his daughter gently

on the head, waved multiple good-byes, then set out for his office in Yoyogi. There'd been no sign that anything was amiss with his daughter since she'd woken in the morning. Her appetite had been normal, and she didn't seem to be in a bad mood. Yet, less than an hour after he dropped her off, he received a call from the daycare informing him his daughter had just died. The words from the president of the daycare didn't immediately sink into his brain. It was impossible to believe a little girl who had just happily waved good-bye to him had died just like that. As she was playing, she had rolled onto her stomach and stopped moving. By the time the caretaker realized something was wrong and walked over, Yoko had already stopped breathing. At first they thought she had died of suffocation, but an autopsy revealed that she had a congenital heart defect.

Fujimura's wife was in a worse state than he was. She blamed herself for going to sleep. It was her day off, she should have been taking care of Yoko herself. If her daughter had been within her reach, it would have never happened. She kept going over the what-ifs, blaming herself, expressing ire over the daycare's slow response.

Nothing was more unbearable to Rieko than hearing about parents losing their children.

"So, your kid now?" she asked.

"Yeah, the next year we had a son."

"Good for you."

"Yeah, but as it turns out, he was born with a weak heart, too, so…"

Rieko was lost for words.

"I mentioned this before, but I played baseball all through junior high and high school and my wife was the captain of the tennis team. I have absolutely no idea how genetics work," he said almost as if he were enjoying the destiny he'd been burdened with.

"How old is he now?"

"He just turned two. He hasn't had a fit yet. Most babies born with heart defects die before their first birthday. They say if he doesn't have an attack by the time he's seven, he can live a relatively normal life."

Rieko suddenly remembered her ex-husband. The man whose gambling habits escalated with the arrival of their daughter overlapped in her mind with Fujimura, who'd left behind an invalid child to come all the way to Shimizu to sleep with someone other than his wife.

"Don't you love your son?" challenged Rieko, despite her readiness to be an accomplice in the affair.

"Of course, I love him very much."

Then why? she almost asked, but held her tongue. Like her husband, this man probably couldn't come up with a decent explanation. She didn't want to hear pretty excuses anyways.

Rieko stood near the wall, rocking back and forth in order to soothe her daughter. Fujimura leaned against the wall next to her. Standing around chatting when they were at her home was rather odd.

"And your wife?" Rieko asked, meaning to inquire about the state of their marriage.

"She's stronger than me," Fujimura said with some force and shook his head.

"You don't like strong women?"

"She's stronger than I am so she doesn't need me."

"Is she still working?"

"No, I guess you could say she's on temporary leave. Now she's at home with the baby, but I think she plans on going back to work."

Rieko wondered about her own situation. Come to think of it, ever since Kiko was just an embryo inside her womb, she felt herself growing stronger by several degrees. It was true that time, too, when five months into her pregnancy she'd been diagnosed with measles. On the way back from seeing the doctor, Rieko and her husband went over the possibility of terminating the pregnancy.

Since her husband simply asked her what she wanted and fell silent, unwilling to share his own views, Rieko, as far as she could recall, pushed her own views on him. According to the doctors, contracting measles during pregnancy meant the baby had a three-in-ten chance of developing a congenital defect of the ears or mouth. A thirty percent chance was very high, and the doctor had delicately suggested that they consider an abortion. Rieko, however, insisted on keeping the baby no matter what. This was their first conception after two and a half years of trying. She feared that it was her only shot at becoming a mother.

In the end, her husband never gave his own opinion, Rieko held to hers, and she gave birth to Kiko.

It was obvious upon birth that Kiko's mouth was normal, but it was impossible to test her hearing until she was out of infancy. When Rieko clapped her hands and called her name, it seemed as though Kiko was reacting. Convincing herself that her baby could hear just fine, Rieko postponed a more thorough evaluation. Deep inside, she was afraid to learn the truth. On the recommendation of her doctor, she finally resolved to have her daughter's hearing abilities tested via EEG. That was when Kiko was revealed to be completely deaf in her right ear, while her left ear suffered a hearing loss of 80 decibels...

Rieko had no choice but to become even stronger upon hearing those results. She bought all the books she could find on hearing impairment and studied intensively. She found an ear doctor and asked him to make every possible effort. She had always wanted to go back to work even if it meant leaving her baby at a daycare, but all her plans needed to change. She decided to dedicate as much time as she could to helping Kiko develop normal speech, speaking to her constantly via her hearing aid. Before she knew, her husband was totally out of her sight and mind.

Whenever anyone asked, Rieko always blamed the divorce on her ex's problem, but the ongoing gambling was the byproduct of a mismatched marriage. She felt the direct cause might be her husband's silence during that period, and her own strength that had brought on that silence. Who was it that had placed a weight on her husband's mouth? It was very likely that he didn't support her decision to have Kiko but couldn't voice his thoughts. He had probably given up from the start, figuring that even if he'd shared his views, Rieko would have overruled him.

Although she was being rocked on her mother's back, Kiko still refused to go to sleep. Her hearing loss had probably made her other senses that much more developed. It was as if she sensed a disturbance in the house's atmosphere and was keeping an eye out to make sure her mother didn't go down the wrong track.

"How could you leave such a beautiful girl?" Fujimura

wondered aloud from her ex's perspective.

"I don't think he thought so."

"I don't believe that."

"Oh, really? Wanna know what he said the last time he saw her? He just spat, 'She's still just a runt.' Can you believe that?"

"No way."

"It's true." Rieko, worn out from standing, sat lightly on the edge of the sofa.

"You seem to like children a lot," she observed, keeping the conversation on the topic of kids as Fujimura, sitting down beside her, made to hug her shoulders.

"No, I had to make an effort to like them," Fujimura replied. He reached out for his glass, not knowing what else to do with his hand.

Fujimura's answer surprised Rieko. Unlike a mother, did a father not feel an immediate outpouring of love for a newborn? Not knowing her daughter was deaf, Rieko never stopped talking to her the nine months she carried her in her womb. No wonder the moment a mother heard her baby's first cries, deep love and excitement overwhelmed her. It was a force that had nothing to do with effort.

"So, you made an effort."

"I don't know. But I did take her to daycare a lot. I liked picking her up a lot better than dropping her off, though."

It seemed cruel to continue asking a man about his dead girl. But Fujimura's expression remained unclouded and his speech was smooth and calm.

"Sounds like you're a good dad."

He demonstrated how he picked her up at the daycare. After greeting the staffer at the entrance, he'd clap twice and call out, "Yoko." His baby girl, playing in a corner of the classroom, would turn around upon hearing her father's voice and gleefully crawl towards the entrance. Fujimura would throw his arms wide open and wait patiently. Her daughter's face would grow bigger and bigger until she lunged into his arms.

As Fujimura described the scene, he reflexively spread out his arms. There was nothing but a glass table in front of his eyes. On it was ice and bottles of whiskey and mineral water. But that wasn't what his eyes were taking in. Rieko didn't doubt that he was seeing the face of his one-year-old daughter recognizing and eagerly approaching him.

"So cute," Fujimura mumbled.

Rieko stared at his profile in disbelief. Were she in his position, she would never have been able to visit her memories with such composure.

Her daughter's weight, which Rieko felt on her back, was real. Every time she turned her head, the sling strap bit painfully into her shoulder. When she imagined losing that presence, what welled up inside her was fear more than sorrow, a pain like her body being ripped to shreds. It wasn't anything so gentle as sorrow.

Suddenly feeling as though she couldn't get enough air, Rieko loosened the sling strap and took a deep breath. She wanted to change the subject as quickly as possible. "Let's have another drink, the three of us."

Arms still weakly held aloft, Fujimura looked as though his mind was still wandering in another dimension, but he came back to his senses when he heard Rieko. "So how's work lately?" he asked, changing the subject himself.

"It's going all right," Rieko nodded. When it came to

whether her boutique was doing well, she could confidently answer in the affirmative. With caring for Kiko taking up so much of her time she couldn't be at the store as much as before, but a partner she'd hired was markedly increasing their sales.

"You must be quite the businesswoman." Apparently having heard how Rieko had transformed her mother's simple sundries store into a first-class boutique, Fujimura was trying to get her to spill the details of her success story.

"It's all thanks to everyone who helped me." Rieko actually believed this—that she had been fortunate. Every time she needed assistance, someone was always there to lend a hand.

Feeling certain that the helpers were men, Fujimura tried to make her confess the number of men she'd been with. His fugue-state gaze from just a moment ago had vanished without a trace and his eyes danced between Rieko's knees and hips. He didn't buy Rieko's assertion that she'd only been with one other man besides her husband prior to her marriage. He warmly admired her body and seemed lost in free fantasies.

It was obvious that raging sexual urges were screaming through Fujimura's body. Rieko found it comical yet flattering at the same time. When he tried to act on his impulses and reached out, Kiko's innocent face blocked his way. Seeing Fujimura retract his hand as if he'd smacked into a wall made Rieko laugh out loud.

"Sorry this didn't turn out the way you expected."

"What do you mean? I came all the way from Tokyo just so we could chat like this."

"Liar."

After two more hours, Kiko still showed no signs of falling asleep. The next day was going to be a rainy Sunday, and neither Rieko nor Fujimura had reason to worry about time. They spoke slowly and unhurriedly about work, children, the future.

Kiko, ever sleepless, had her eyes wide open keeping watch. In this test of endurance, it seemed Fujimura didn't stand a chance. His very desire was on the verge of wilting.

Then, just as soon as the man stopped seeing the woman as a sexual object, the distance between them mysteriously shrank. Liberated from his one-track thought process, Fujimura was able to focus on better understanding his companion.

The rain was still pouring, and even with the space heater cranked high it didn't do much to warm the room.

Kiko fell asleep with a nearly audible thud. It was almost dawn. It had been quite a long while since Rieko had conversed with a man until daybreak. Even with her ex, she'd never stayed up until dawn just to talk. She wondered for a moment if their both having a disabled child had kept the conversation going. That was true about her ex, too, so she didn't think that was the reason.

They stood up pretty much simultaneously.

"Let's get some sleep."

Two futon sets were laid out in one of the tatami rooms.

Kiko slept breathing softly on Rieko's right, and Fujimura, changed into pajamas, lay on her left.

"Your efforts were in vain. Sorry, Mr. Babysitter from Tokyo," intoned Rieko, trying to stifle a laugh.

"The whole time I was driving to Shimizu from Tokyo,

I was standing at attention."

"You can drive standing?" Rieko asked, absurdly, not grasping his meaning.

Fujimura gave her some time to process his remark, leaving it up to her imagination.

"Oh, God. Don't say things like that in front of the baby."

"Yep, stood the whole way here, after I stopped on Tomei to call you. I thought about you the whole time. And that's not all. I've been up these past five days, every day and night. You're killing me." It looked as though he really was in agony. "Killing me..." he repeated three more times. "I'm so exhausted from being up all the time that I've gone limp."

"Silly."

Sleep was sneaking up. Rieko turned towards Fujimura and asked, "Hey, can I put my feet in?"

Fujimura didn't respond.

He probably wasn't sure what she meant, so she explained, "I have poor blood circulation. My feet stay frozen even when they're under the covers."

"Go ahead," Fujimura said, his voice gone sleepy. Rieko moved so her body was at an angle and stuck her lower legs under his covers. Her feet must have been icy because he gave a small jolt, but he covered her feet with his calves to gently warm them. This was the first time their skins had touched.

"Come hang out again, Mr. Foot Warmer."

There was no reply. Fujimura was already fast asleep. Even though she had made the first move, he was slumbering after simply warming her feet. She tried wiggling her toes to tickle his calf, but there was no reaction. His leg muscles were completely soft.

His sleep breathing, at first regular, was soon interrupted by rough snoring. Rieko reached out above her pillow and groped about in the darkness until she could slide open the window and storm shutter a crack. She sat up. The watery rays of morning sunlight gave Fujimura's face a pallid hue. His snoring didn't seem like it would subside anytime soon. Kiko slept peacefully, utterly undisturbed by the noise, but Rieko wasn't so lucky. She was strangely wakeful, so she leaned on her elbow and stared into Fujimura's face for a while.

Utterly exhausted, he slept like a log. His brows were deeply furrowed, and occasionally he mumbled something from his slackened lips. He had to have been making efforts to appear cheerful while he was awake. Asleep and unguarded, true emotions came to the fore, the heart mercilessly writ on the dreamer's visage. His brimmed with suffering. What was he dreaming about? Who was he seeing?

Rieko burrowed under the futon until it covered her shoulders and lay on her back. She wasn't sleepy anymore—not because of the snoring, but because Fujimura's grieving heart kept snagging her attention and keeping drowsiness at bay. If it were possible, she wanted to salve his wounds, even a little. It crossed her mind that if they'd embraced, naked, his face might have been a little more tranquil.

Fujimura died on Wednesday, four days later. Before she could feel any shock, Rieko recalled the expression on his face early in his sleep. Manifestly, his vitality had seemed to be receding. Perhaps for that reason, when his employer, the apparel manufacturer, called to inform her that he had died in an accident, Rieko found herself strangely accepting of the news.

They gave her the new sales rep's name, and she offered some vague reply and hung up. After a while, though, growing curious about the circumstances of Fujimura's death, she called back the company to find out the time and place of the accident.

On the first Tuesday of every month, Rieko took her daughter to a university hospital in Tokyo for a checkup. Rather than exams per se, it functioned more like a counseling session full of useful info for a parent with a hearing-impaired child. Rieko hadn't missed a single session yet, and the next one was next Tuesday. Fujimura's accident scene was fairly close to the university hospital. She should have enough time to lay some flowers. While they had only spent a single night in each other's company, she could still vividly recall his warm legs. She felt it was somehow her duty to see where exactly that warmth had been snuffed out.

Once March rolled around, the weather suddenly became spring-like and the days grew calm. On her previous trip to Tokyo the month before, it had been terribly cold and rainy, and she'd been forced to use taxis throughout to make her way around the city. With the first signs of spring, though, it felt like walking around an unfamiliar city a little might be nice. At around 2 p.m., after the checkup counseling, Rieko took a cab to Senzokuike, looked for a florist, and headed to the location of the accident on foot.

Fujimura's accident had occurred a week ago on the first gentle left-hand curve past Ring Road No. 7.

As Rieko pushed the stroller, Kiko's head lolled back and forth. Listening to the faint sounds of an unfamiliar place through her hearing aid, she was on the verge of falling into her afternoon nap.

"After turning from Ring Road No. 7 onto Nakahara Street, you'll see a big furniture store. It happened right in front of it," Fujimura's boss had said, tactfully explaining the geography.

Before Rieko even noticed the furniture store, she spotted a bouquet of flowers at the foot of a tree along the edge of the road. There it was, the exact site of the accident. The flowers were already wilting. If they'd been left shortly after the accident, they'd have been doused in gas fumes for a week. After placing her newly purchased bouquet beside the old one, Rieko pressed her hands together before her face.

It's a gentle curve, but there were no skid marks from the brakes...

Those words had kept coming back to her and made her want to see the site herself. Fujimura's car had left no streaks on the road prior to crossing over the center line and slamming head-first into an oncoming truck. It was past eleven in the evening but he hadn't been drinking. Rieko couldn't help but wonder about Fujimura's death.

He suffered severe blunt force trauma. He died almost instantly.

He hadn't been wearing a seatbelt.

She stood on the curbstone so she could see the left-hand curve from Fujimura's point of view. On that weekday afternoon, Nakahara Street bustled with traffic, but when the flow of cars periodically halted in sync with the lights, the yellow center line stood out distinctly. The street curved gently to the left on a slight slope. She imagined the street at night. Past eleven, traffic would be sparse. Illuminated by headlights, the center line was a boundary separating the world into this side and that side. What did Fujimura see beyond the yellow line?

Rieko suspected that he might have committed suicide. Maybe "suicide" was too strong a word. He probably just made a simple mistake while driving his car. Yet, she felt like she'd glimpsed his temptation, his sudden desire to cross that line. Two weeks ago on Saturday, he'd had the chance to make love to Rieko but had fallen fast asleep instead. Might the black thing that had sidelined his sexual urge, that same perverse temptation, inserted itself into his driving?

Grief over losing a child would persist deep down no matter how cheerfully one behaved on the surface. His son, too, had been born with a congenital heart defect. The same tragedy could easily repeat itself.

Rieko shook her head. She tried putting herself in Fujimura's position, but her mind furiously turned down the attempt—it was too tortuous even to imagine.

They came for him, Rieko mumbled to herself. Then it struck her—maybe they didn't "come" for him, but he had "gone" instead. Fujimura hadn't been able to pick up his daughter after dropping her off at the daycare. He was now clapping, calling out "Yoko" and spreading his arms wide, most likely picking her up on the far side. She had no trouble picturing Fujimura's face as he hugged close his approaching daughter.

May he be beaming as he embraces her, Rieko prayed.

She felt a sense of satisfaction at having seen something through to the end. She walked back down the street and hailed a cab right before the intersection. She collapsed the stroller and held her sleeping baby in her arms, climbed into the backseat, and told the driver her destination.

"Tokyo station, please."

181

After the taxi made the gentle curve, thanks to the slight slope Rieko could see a patch of blue sky peeking through the windshield.

Avidya

I parked the car on the side of the road simply because I wanted to see the color of the water. The route had a succession of gentle curves, and even driving slowly, glancing down at the river would have compromised my focus. I decided it would be safer as well as more time-efficient to stop instead and have a good look at the river.

After the Chuo Expressway's Ina Interchange exit, the road split into northbound and southbound routes. The former led to Chino, and the latter through Hasemura and Misakubo, eventually intersecting with the Tokaido corridor. Our destination was a log cabin, apparently built on the remains of an abandoned school, in a settlement known as Ura located near the Southern Alps past Hasemura. Soon after turning south, one could see the long, thin Sanbi Reservoir stretched out along the dam. Running parallel to the road, the lake-like reservoir eventually thinned into a narrow river. There was a sign for the Mibu River before the bridge, and the character for "bu," meaning peak, had aroused my curiosity as to the color of the water.

My two daughters in the backseat had apparently fallen asleep simultaneously, and I could hear the sounds of their even breathing. Just a short while ago, the car had been filled with their high-pitched chatter as the eldest, having just entered elementary school, read out the phonetic spelling of every single sign and shop name she could see out the window, while her sister, just four years old, parroted everything. Their voices were earsplitting, and no matter how many times I scolded them for being noisy, there wasn't a single minute of silence.

When I turned back to glance between the seats I saw my daughters fast asleep, collapsed on top of each other. My wife, trapped in the back seat with her chest and knees pinned underneath the girls in what must have been an uncomfortable position, stared at a map. She directed a tired-looking face towards me, seemingly unperturbed by the sudden stop.

"I'm just getting out for a second to take a look," I stated and got out of the car.

The heat outside was intense. The cicadas cried in chorus, the sound traveling from the surrounding mountains into the valley below like an avalanche, loud enough that the swaying of the undergrowth in the cedar forest seemed a response. Indeed, it was strange to see the rustling in the absence of wind. As I got closer to the riverbank and glanced down on the water, gooseflesh rose up across my body. This area near the foot of the Southern Alps lacked the aura of a sacred place, yet even the hairs on my cheeks stood on end. I felt apprehensive as if I sensed something on the other side of the mountains. With such thoughts in mind I surveyed the water's color. Since the fountainhead was in Mt. Senjo the water was very clear, but it was just an ordinary blue hue. Last year and the year before, when I rode my motorcycle from Yoshino to Kumano through the pass at Mt. Omine, the color of the water as it meandered along the bottom of the ravine was a vibrant green. It could have been the water itself or components of the stones on the riverbed that imparted the tint, but only in the depths of the Kii Peninsula did water reveal such a mysterious color.

Since then, whenever I drive through mountains and happen upon a river, I stop to check the color, but I have yet to see water as profound, limpid, and green.

I went back to the car and closed the door, accidentally using too much force and slamming it shut. I turned back to check for a reaction from my daughters, but they showed no sign of waking. Since leaving the apartment in Tokyo early in the morning they'd been carrying on quite boisterously, so it was no wonder they were now deep asleep.

"I wonder how much longer we have to go," my wife inquired about the remaining time on our journey, probably sensing that our destination was close at hand.

"We'll be there within the hour," I answered, glancing at the clock on the dashboard. It was just past 3:00 p.m.

"We have to get there by five," my wife insisted, worried about not getting there in time to prep dinner.

"Don't worry, we've got plenty of time."

"Really?"

"So long as we don't get lost."

The kindergarten my elder daughter had attended had about fifty students per class. Because of the relatively small size, many of the parents actively mingled with one another, and every summer a volunteer group of guardians led a several-days-long trip where the kids learned how to cook. My elder girl had graduated and entered elementary school that April; some families moved away and others were enrolled in different elementary schools, and we feared that these parental activities would cease. But since we had an organizer and volunteers, the Camp School was able to continue. This year, the organizer, who happened to be my former colleague and a good friend, lent us all his log cabin so we could hold the camp for three nights and four days. Due to work, however, our family had to make our way there a day later than everyone else.

The other five families had already arrived at the campground the day before. As this was the first time the cabin would be used this summer, they were likely hard at work cleaning the interior and preparing the cast-iron heated bathtubs. It would be awkward for us to arrive just in time to eat dinner after the other families had done all the work. I could understand why my wife wanted to get there in time to help cook dinner, at least.

"Hey, can you navigate?" I had the directions from Ina Interchange to that point memorized, but standard maps were useless when it came to navigating the narrow mountain roads that lay ahead.

"I'll try," she replied without confidence. We had yet to reach our destination without issue when my wife, who had no sense of direction, navigated.

We'd received a fax with the directions to the cabin a few days ago. In the margins had been a warning: "There are zero landmarks in the area. Please be careful when you make your way here."

Avidya

According to the standard map, after the small settlement, the road simply vanished. A road doesn't necessarily link one location to another. Like a river whose source was hidden in the mountains, a road could get swallowed up by a range and disappear. The standard map didn't even indicate the settlement's name, and I only learned the name "Ura" for the first time on the fax. My friend said he'd built his cabin on the site of an abandoned school outside the settlement right where the road ended on the map. I was seized by curiosity. As it was located on the western foot of Mt. Senjo, I anticipated sensing the spirit of the mountain.

Two summers ago, I felt what was referred to as the spirit of a mountain for the first time. After reading a piece that described Tenkawa Village in Oku Yoshino in a book I'd happened to pick up, I decided to go on a solo motorcycle tour.

I took the ferry from Cape Irago across to Toba and took Route 42 down to Owase, then a turn deep into the mountainous terrain of the Kii Peninsula. It was bright and sunny the whole time I rode along the coast of Kumano Nada, but as I climbed the winding mountain roads and rose in altitude, clouds descended on the summits, blocking out the sun as if the previous good weather had been nothing but a dream. The locals claimed that the weather was always fickle in those parts. Even if it was sunny downhill, they said, you were practically guaranteed to run into rain as you went into the hills.

The rain came out of nowhere and suddenly moved on without settling in any particular location. Putting on and removing my rain gear became a hassle, so every time I encountered a squall I stowed the motorcycle under a dense thicket and took shelter. That was why I wasn't making much progress. My plan was to arrive in Tenkawa by 5:00 p.m. and to find a convenient lodging for the night. Just as I started to feel anxious over wasting so much time, I found a signpost that seemed to indicate a shortcut to the village. According to the map, the road turned into a tunnel that ran under Mt. Gyojagaeshi and went straight to Tenkawa. It seemed to pierce right through the center of the Omine Range, which was comprised of Mt. Sanjo, Mt. Daifugen, Mt. Yayama, Mt. Bukkyo, and Mt. Shaka. On the map the road was not marked red or green, which would indicate a national highway or main thoroughfare, but yellow, which meant it was a rough, unpaved mountain road. It was definitely a shortcut, but there was a risk I wouldn't be able to pass through with a bike built for ordinary roads. I stood straddling the seat and contemplated my choices for a minute, standing right at the fork. But the decision was already made before I had time to puzzle over it—I needed to commit to moving forward. If I got stuck, I'd deal with it then. I could always turn back. I mentally readied myself and turned left.

The road condition worsened the farther uphill I traveled, and branches that leaned out into the road repeatedly scratched at my elbows and shoulders. It was quite narrow, barely wide enough for a single car to pass through. There was no oncoming traffic nor any vehicles in my rearview mirror. If I had an accident and fell into the ravine, I'd probably disappear from the world without anyone ever finding me. In fact, the bottom of the ravine must have held countless souls of travelers who had fallen in the middle of their journeys. The place had an aura that rose up unannounced that gave credence to such notions.

Large rocks were strewn across the road and the ground

water sprang up from the mountainside and flowed swiftly across the road. I had to maintain a slow pace and pay constant attention to the surface. Even at such a snail-like speed I had probably covered about ten miles. Right before the Gyojagaeshi tunnel, just as I thought the stream on the right side had vanished, I discovered a landslide that blocked the road at an angle. Right at a curve in the road, the stream disappeared, buried under earth and rocks. I slammed on the brakes just in time, got off the bike, and walked closer. It seemed as if the Earth's skin had been turned inside out. The roots of plants stuck upwards, and soil bulged high, squashing the small stream. It seemed like the landslide had happened recently as the surface of the soil still looked damp, and the smell of wet dirt traveled all the way into my helmet. It was then that I understood why there had been no oncoming cars. All traffic was cut off.

Tenkawa lay just on the other side of the tunnel right before me. The frustration that I felt diminished my desire to resume my trip. In order to pull myself together, I took off my gloves and helmet, rolled my shoulders, and took deep breaths. Just as I switched off the ignition and shut down the engine, silent mountain spirits descended.

Clouds hovered over the northwestern sky above the mountain ridge, making the leaves on the trees rustle with falling rain, while the southern sky had only a thin layer of clouds where soft sunlight filtered through the gaps. All of the overlapping light and dark clouds moved briskly.

All of a sudden, the trees in the nearby forest swayed. A warm wind blew down through the virgin woods, a mix of evergreen and deciduous trees whose roots were covered with bamboo grasses. The wind that passed through the dark, lush foliage was steeped in the smell of trees, soil, and water. A presence filled the flowing air that made me shiver, and my skin burst into gooseflesh. I stepped into the untouched forest and parted the branches to look up towards the summit. I saw a stream of gray rubble, the texture of which was totally different from the surrounding soil, snaking up the hill. Water flowed abundantly from all over, yet this particular strand of rubble appeared to be a dry riverbed. For a while I was frozen to the spot as if I'd been cursed by the mountain spirits or by the presence of gods. As I stared at the mountaintop I felt a powerful desire bubbling up inside me: If there in fact was a mysterious entity living on the top of the mountain, I wanted to walk up the ridge and come into contact with it until I'd had my fill.

One would think I'd have retraced my steps and taken a detour after running into a landslide right before reaching Tenkawa, but that wasn't what happened. If I took the long way around, I'd have had to travel at least another sixty miles, which would waste over two hours. As the crow flies, my destination was right in front of me, just past the collapsed earth. The thought of giving up and turning back vexed me, so I decided to look for another option.

The landslide had tumbled onto the road towards the valley, skimming across the edge and stopping right where a few dead trees lay blocking the dry riverbed. I tried walking up the side of the mountain where the slide had occurred to try to cross over to the other side and to Tenkawa. As I was terrified of falling back into the valley, I leaned into the side of the mountain, using my hands as crutches as I climbed. Here and there large boulders lay exposed, their surfaces wet and slippery, but they were close, only about five yards apart. I could easily cross over on foot. If I could just leave the bike, there wouldn't be a problem, but I couldn't quite do that. I walked back and forth several times, checking the stability of the ground, kicking away any exposed rocks. If it was possible to cross over, I wanted to. It wasn't in my nature to just give up and skulk away. Being single-minded, and gradually finding myself able to walk up the hill without using my hands, I was seized with the absurd idea of riding over on my bike.

But as soon as I glanced down into the valley, I lost heart. The rocks that I kicked over clattered along the dry riverbed and rolled until they were no longer visible and kept on falling, the noise of their descent echoing through the trees. If I lost my balance and fell with my bike, there was no telling how far I would tumble down the mountain. But if I kept my eyes away from the ravine and bore ahead with the same momentum as if it were a log bridge... If I didn't mess up, I would reach the other side. That was my judgment.

Later on when I told my wife about this experience, she screamed, *What if you'd fallen into the ravine? Stop being so reckless!* Of course, it was only because I'd made it to the other side safely that I could tell my wife a slightly embellished version of my mini-adventure in the mountains. But bragging about the thrill and my sense of triumph was silly and immature, and my wife spoke as though she were scolding a rambunctious little boy. Indeed, had I fallen, it would have been too much for my wife to bear. How was she supposed to wait for a husband who'd vanished during a motorcycle trip as though he'd been spirited away? No wonder she was livid.

I stopped the car near the bridge because my wife had said, "Wait, hold on a second. I might've made a mistake." It seemed that we were on the wrong road, and even if we wanted to ask for directions there were no houses in sight. "Let's go a little further. I'll go ask someone if we find a house."

I doubted we'd find any houses this deep in the mountains, but I crossed the bridge and continued up the road as my wife suggested. Shortly thereafter, we came across a house that resembled a smoke hut. My wife jumped out of the car and ran in and dragged out an old man dressed in fieldworker's clothes. As my wife spoke ceaselessly at him, he pointed back down the hill we'd just ascended. I couldn't hear what they were saying through the closed car window, but the old man's gestures seemed to indicate that we'd been driving along the wrong road. After getting directions, my wife bowed to the old man a few times, ran back to the car, and bowed again as she opened the door.

"We shouldn't have crossed that bridge," my wife informed me, catching her breath.

"But there were no other roads."

"No, he says there's a narrow road that goes uphill right before the bridge. We couldn't see it because we were going downhill."

"Okay…"

There was no space to make a U-turn, but since it wasn't that far, I decided to reverse until we got to the edge of the bridge. The old man who had helped us with directions came to the front of the car, watching us with a worried look. I wondered what he was worried about. Was it for the safety of us city slickers? About whether we'd reach our intended destination? He was still motioning, waving a finger to the left. He meant that we had to take a left before the bridge. Even as the old man receded into the distance, he continued to energetically wave left. I noted a resemblance. Thanks to the angular line of his chin in particular, reminiscent of a stone statue of the Buddha, he overlapped in my mind with an ascetic I'd met at the end of June that year on the summit of Mt. Shaka in the Omine Range.

Having toured the Omine Range for two years in a row, my fascination with the area had deepened. I was deeply curious to discover with my own eyes the holy entity that lived on the top of the mountain, the source that breathed out the spiritually charged wind that wended through the virgin woods. When I saw literature in a bookstore about Yoshino and Kumano I'd pick it up and flip through, and if it piqued my interest I bought it in order to broaden my knowledge. One study of folklore described Mt. Omine as the birthplace of the Shugendo practice, and naturally, recalling the aura of the place, my interest expanded to include ascetic hermits and mountain worship. I wanted to go again, this time to the peak.

At long last I was able to take four days off at the end of June that year to realize my dreams. In fact, I had wanted to take part in the ascetic training hosted by the monks of Mt. Omine Temple that included walking the Omine-Okugake pilgrimage path, but it involved staying in the mountains for four nights. The path was fifty miles long, requiring at least a week to traverse, which wasn't possible with my schedule, so my only option was to scale the mountain on my own. I was supposed to start a new job on July 1st, my first time back in full-time employment in six years.

During the previous six years, after quitting the event production company I'd worked for, I hadn't stuck with a regular job. My wife and I both worked, but with the arrival of our first daughter, one of us had to quit or change careers. Even if we left our daughter at a daycare, they were only open from 9 a.m. to 5 p.m., so we'd have been forced to pay for two-fold childcare. Whereas my wife had a stable income as a school librarian, the event production company I worked for was on the verge of writing rubber checks. So I yielded and said goodbye to the life of a salaryman for a while. Since quitting the publishing company I joined fresh out of college, I'd lost count of the times I'd switched occupations. Others probably saw me as a lazy bum who couldn't hold down a job, but I was full of vim and vigor and saw taking on new jobs in new fields as a challenge. Perhaps that's why I hardly balked at the idea of becoming a stay-at-home dad.

Taking my daughters back and forth from daycare every day and handling the majority of the childrearing duties and chores, I also put to use my physical strength, honed through judo in junior high and high school, to work as a personal trainer at a gym whenever I had free time. I had spent the past six years as both stay-at-home dad and part-time employee. It was significantly easier to have a salaried position, but what I gained during that period was significant. Bathing my daughters, washing their dirty cloth diapers, yelling in frustration over minor and major bathroom accidents, swinging between joy and despair over their behavior... The duress of raising the kids myself created a bond between us beyond the dreams of a father who could only play with his children during his free time, which in turn made my wife place even greater trust in me.

Attachment to those closest to oneself is a source of energy. The year before, when I entered a local weightlifting tournament and was on the verge of winning the competition with a 330-lb bar bell, I imagined my daughters about to be crushed by a megalith. I needed to lift it if I wanted to save them. That split-second image determined the outcome of the competition. The importance of family was no empty credo for me. I threw myself into increasing my physical strength as if to compensate for the small income I brought to the household and in order to be prepared for worst-case scenarios.

My daughters were bigger now, the elder in elementary school and the younger just turned four. They took up much less of my time, and furthermore the daycare my younger girl attended had recently expanded their hours of operation. Just as I felt it was an opportune time to go back to work, my former boss at the publishing company called to ask if I was interested in helping out at a new publishing packager he was setting up. That was in the beginning of June. By the middle of that month, spurred on by my wife, I told my former boss that I'd be honored to work for him again and made various arrangements so that I could start commuting to the office on July 1st. Since I wouldn't be able to take a holiday for a while once I started the new job, I asked my wife if I could take the four last days of June as a break just for myself. She graciously consented, under one condition: that I would not be reckless.

I decided to take the Tomei Expressway out to Hamamatsu, and from Cape Irago I'd take a ferry to Toba. On the way back I'd take Route 25 and the Higashi Meihan Expressway to Nagoya, and from there take the Tomei back home.

I would ride my bike up to the base of the mountain trail then leave the machine behind during the ascent. In order to use the four days to the fullest, considering the trek to and from the mountains, I decided a motorbike had the best mobility. The problem was deciding on which mountain within the Omine Range to climb from Yoshino: Mt. Sanjo, Mt. Daifugen, Mt. Yayama, Mt. Bukkyo, Mt. Kujaku, or Mt. Shaka. I would need four days to cross the entire span of the mountains, which wasn't a possibility. Even if I chose two or three mountains and left the bike at the base and summited, at best I'd be able to spend only one night in a cabin on the peak. There were two options: a pilgrim's lodge on Mt. Sanjo and a hut on Mt. Yayama. Were I to spend the night at the foot of Mt. Sanjo, that to this day prohibits women, I would have to stay in Yoshino, but the guidebook stated that the path from Yoshino to the top of Mt. Sanjo was a gentle slope all the way. On the other hand, if I stayed in the pilgrim's lodge in Zenkiguchi at the foot of Mt. Shaka, hiking to Mt. Yayama and back would offer magnificent views. I'd be able to get right above the Gyojagaeshi tunnel, previously blocked off by the landslide, and through an area where Oyama magnolias grew wild. I wanted to take the more precipitous path, which meant my only choice was the latter route, which automatically decided where I would stay for the three nights. I would be lodging at an inn at the base, the hut on Mt. Yayama, and the pilgrim's lodge in Zenkiguchi in between. Only the first required a reservation—the others would house me so long as I managed to get there.

Ten hours after leaving Tokyo, I arrived at the inn at 5:00 p.m. I took a long bath to relax my muscles after the long touring and made preparations for the next days' hike. As it was a weekday at the end of June, there were no other visitors. The place was so quiet it seemed that after dinner there was nothing else to do but go back to my room and sleep. I think I was in bed by nine.

The next day, I rose early, ate breakfast, took three rice balls and a thermos filled with tea, and left the inn. After arriving at the Zenkiguchi pilgrim's lodge, I abandoned the bike and prepared for the hike. I removed my leather boots and changed into thick-soled sneakers. I grabbed the backpack strapped to the rear and tied a white cloth around my head.

At six in the morning, blue patches could be glimpsed in parts of the sky, but as the mountain weather was fickle, I had to diligently prepare rain gear. As it was my first time summiting, I had no clue as to the pace I needed to maintain to reach the hut on Mt. Yayama by evening. I had more than enough energy. Yet, I knew taking this mountain lightly was like begging for trouble as it was a holy peak with an aura unique enough to merit the title of sacred precinct. The inn owner had told me a story about a man plagued by spirits and lured down divergent paths who was never heard from again. *Don't do anything reckless,* I repeated to myself over and over as I climbed the dry riverbed that ran parallel to a mountain stream.

The path meandered upwards. Around seven, a light fog settled in. Out of nowhere in particular, I could hear noises that could have been raindrops or branch tips brushing together. I stopped every time I heard it to gaze in the direction of the sound. If it was rain, I needed to take my rain gear out of my backpack, as occasionally a drenching squall would pass through these parts.

I strained my ears, but it didn't seem to be rain.

Apparently raindrops or dew left on the leaves were getting tossed about by wind and the supple tree trunks were amplifying the sound. I decided to pay it no heed and climb on. I passed through a pair of giant boulders called Futatsu Iwa. By the time I reached Taiko-no-Tsuji, the terminus for the time being of the uphill path, it was nine. That meant I'd been walking through the precipitous terrain without a proper rest break for three hours.

By that time my shirt and sweatshirt were soaked with sweat and I was gasping for breath. There, I encountered a man around sixty, apparently a Shugendo ascetic, sitting on a rock and staring at the opening of the mountain trail. He was garbed in traditional mountain ascetic attire—a white *suzukake* robe, wide *hakama* pants, split-toed socks with heavy soles, a kerchief on his head. He held a *khakkhara* ringed staff, and a goatskin pelt for sitting was strapped to his backside.

I was surprised to be greeted by him as if he'd known all along that I'd be climbing up there. As soon as I met his gaze in order to return the greeting, his face broke into a giant smile. He called out in a loud, jolly voice, but I couldn't make out what he was saying. Perhaps he was speaking in a local dialect since I couldn't understand a single word. I nodded silently in reply and slowly made my way closer to the rock on which the ascetic sat. He said a few more words, and still I couldn't comprehend him. I decided to offer a conventional greeting.

"Hello."

The ascetic indicated the spot next to him on the rock. "You did well coming up here," the man approved joyfully.

This time I got what he was saying. His words were suddenly registering in my brain as if my ear pressure had just normalized and my hearing had been restored.

"Where to?" I inquired after his destination as I sat down on the rock.

"What? Oh, I'm just here to greet."

I wasn't entirely sure of his meaning. Did he mean he was sitting here greeting all hikers from Zenkiguchi one by one, or did he have some sort of religious reason?

Perhaps sensing my confusion he explained, "A group of pilgrims walking the Omine-Okugake route is scheduled to pass here around noon."

I finally understood. Fifty or so Shugendo practitioners who had left Yoshino two days prior had crossed Mt. Sanjo and Mt. Yayama and would be passing here around noon on their way back to Zenkiguchi along the trail I'd just climbed. The ascetic further explained that he traveled up the mountain the same day each year to that very spot to greet pilgrims, to show appreciation for their efforts, and to give them encouragement for the final bit of their journey.

Since ancient times, the "ordered peaks" route for the Omine-Okugake pilgrimage had been to walk from the Kumano Sanzan shrines across the Omine mountain range to Yoshino. The opposite route, from Yoshino through the Omine mountain range to Kumano Sanzan, was called "reverse peaks." Nowadays, most Omine-Okugake pilgrims walked the "reverse peaks" route, while the other one that went from Yoshino through Mt. Yayama over the mountain ridge and ending here in Taiko-no-Tsuji had fallen into disuse. Further south past that point, Mt. Tengu, Mt. Jizo, Mt. Nehan, and Mt. Kasasute were impregnable, without so much as an animal trail, so the pilgrims had no choice but to go downhill to Zenkiguchi from Taiko-no-Tsuji.

After I asked the man for directions to Mt. Yayama, he looked me over with narrowed eyes. "With your body, you'd probably get there in eight hours."

Eight hours from now meant I could get to the hut by 5 p.m. Even so, I didn't feel like resting for much longer, partly because I worried the ascetic may have overestimated the strength of my legs.

"Well, I should get going now." I stood and bowed, and started out towards Mt. Dainichi. The ascetic retrieved two staffs from the clump of bushes behind his rock, tucked them under his elbows, and stood up. Until then, I hadn't noticed the two staffs hidden in the bushes.

"I'll come with you a short ways." He stepped in front of me and started walking. He planted the two staffs on the ground before him, swung both legs through the air, and landed in a crouch. I was so stunned that I stopped walking.

"Something the matter?" the ascetic asked, looking back. I tried to continue walking as if nothing had happened, but I was so agitated that I couldn't take a step. Had I seen this manner of locomotion in the world down below, it wouldn't have affected me. But we were right next to Mt. Dainichi, which was over 6,500 feet above sea level. It was an arduous climb to the summit even for those in tip-top shape. When I thought of the treacherous trail I'd just taken from Zenki-guchi, I was overwhelmed by what I was witnessing. Both of his legs were clearly prosthetics from the hip down, which meant that he had come all this way relying only on the strength of his two arms and the staffs.

As I followed behind him, I gradually began to accept the

fact. The two staffs held fast against his elbows had become a part of his body, and he could easily avoid any obstacles along the path. His movements were determined and nimble as if to reject any helping hands that might be proffered. Whether he had lost his legs earlier in life or it had been congenital, he emanated a powerful commitment to overcome the fate he'd been burdened with. Watching him negotiate the humus with his staffs instead of his feet cheered my heart bit by bit.

The ascetic and I went separate ways at Jinsen-no-Shuku, the midway point between Mt. Dainichi and Mt. Shaka, and I entered the steep climb up Mt. Shaka alone. The ascetic loitered there for a while, glancing up the path, and waved boldly at me before retracing his steps. We had promised to see each other again after I returned to the Zenkiguchi pilgrim's lodge two days later.

The first couple of hours were always the toughest part of a climb, but after that I found my pace and had an easier time of it. It took about an hour to get from Jinsen-no-Shuku to the peak of Mt. Shaka. I kept up a pretty brisk pace just as the ascetic had predicted.

"With your legs, you'd be there in about an hour," he'd said encouragingly before we parted.

By noon the fog had completely lifted, and from the summit I could look down through the sparsely forested mountain ridges into the valleys below. A cluster of strangely shaped stones stood exposed on the bare mountain surface. After I stared at them for a while, each started to look like a statue of the Buddha.

Suddenly, I heard a sound like someone was blowing a conch shell in the distance. When I listened intently, I noted that after the conch shell a group of people chanted Buddhist prayers in unison. The voices seemed to be coming from different places, changing with the shifting wind, but the general direction was from Mt. Yayama, my destination. A group of Omine-Okugake pilgrims were apparently on their way as the ascetic had mentioned.

From the shadow of a boulder appeared a man with neat features, beads pressed between his palms and in front of his face in prayer-pose. He was the officiating monk leading the pilgrims.

Three Shugendo practitioners that followed him blew on conch shells simultaneously, stood at the base of the trail, and called out in robust voices: "Repent, repent."

"Purify the six senses," the other pilgrims chanted in response.

Repent, repent, purify the six senses.
Repent, repent, purify the six senses.

The fifty pilgrims repeated the call-and-response prayer countless times as they summited the mountain. The six senses referred to in the Buddhist prayer were sight, hearing, smell, taste, touch, and consciousness—the sum total of body and mind that makes up a person. The idea was that offering penitence and sharpening and purifying the senses humans were endowed with led to becoming one with the spirit of the mountain. Panting as they climbed, the pilgrims prayed, imbuing the chant with their own thoughts, and one by one reached the peak. They bowed slightly when our eyes met, and I returned with an inclination of my head. As if to greet all the pilgrims on their way to see the

Sakyamuni statue on the peak, I stood there for twenty minutes. Once they surrounded the Sakyamuni statue in a circle, the monk led them in a recital of the Heart Sutra.

Maka Hannya Haramita Shin Gyo

Kanjizai bosatsu,
gyojin hannya haramitta ji,
shoken goon kaiku,
do issai kuyaku, Sha-ri-shi:
shiki fui ku, ku fui shiki,
shiki sokuze ku, ku sokuze shiki

Garbed entirely white, the pilgrims rubbed their prayer beads, kept rhythm by shaking their *khakkhara*, and poured their various thoughts into the Heart Sutra as they recited it. As I watched from behind, I had the urge to try and peek into every pilgrim's heart. I wondered what they were praying for, what sins they were burdened with. Below the goatskin pelts slung across their backsides, their pant legs smeared with mud told of the treacherous journey they'd undertaken. What was it that they were trying to gain through so much effort?

Before arriving in the mountains, I had read a number of books explaining the Heart Sutra to get the general gist of its sense. It was the most common prayer recited on Mt. Omine, and I was also curious to know what was written in a short sutra of only 263 Japanese characters.

The world is emptiness. The components that comprise man's body and awareness—eyes, ears, nose, tongue, body, and mind—do not exist. Nothing is created, and therefore nothing can be destroyed. There is no impurity nor purity, no increase nor decrease. Therefore, since there "is" nothing, one should relinquish all attachments. That way the human heart can be freed from suffering, and peace will visit one's heart... I interpret the first part as such. There are many things I can't swallow if it ends there. If "life" engenders suffering and has to be relinquished to annul suffering, how are humans supposed to lead their current lives? Do people have to live as if they're dead? Accepting for a moment that "life" means stepping into mud, shouldn't one keep going once the first step is taken? Not teaching the way to go on and instead declaring that neither this nor that "is" seems, well, pointless.

But the Heart Sutra doesn't fail to offer a helping hand in its coda. A mantra meant to ease all suffering:

Gaté Gaté Paragaté Parasamgaté, Bodhi Svaha!

It's the only section of the Heart Sutra, originally a mixture of Sanskrit and Pali, that was simply transliterated for the Japanese version. Translating it, they must have feared, risked stripping away the sonority of the original and thereby its miraculous efficacy. Of course, religious figures have attempted to render the line in Japanese. As long as it retains the essential meaning, it's a free for all.

Go, go, together to cross there, blessed be enlightenment!

Many religious figures interpret its sense thus.

I can't get rid of the impression that the sutra suddenly changes its tone at that point. Up until then, it's been denying that anything "is," but all of a sudden it's "go," which almost sounds encouraging. The world is filled with all manner of suffering, including the four inevitabilities of life—birth, aging, sickness, and death—and while it may feel meaningless to keep on living, the mantra says to "go" anyways. No matter how cruel life may be, the world is still filled with beauty. The living cannot afford to be just pure. Drag your legs or even crawl if necessary, but go through this transient world. After that, one will surely attain enlightenment.

The Shugendo practitioners were chanting the final mantra of the Heart Sutra:

Gaté Gaté Paragaté Parasamgaté, Bodhi Svaha...

Their voices grew louder all at once, their hands gripping their *khakkhara* tighter. They were commanding their own hearts, and their thoughts floated on the wind, traveling down the exposed mountain surface and wending between the trees. This, without a doubt, was what I'd sensed on the road along the foothills on the trip I'd taken two summers ago.

The car climbed the uphill road, a succession of steep curves.

"Hm? What?" my wife asked.

I glanced at the rearview mirror to look at the back seat. "What do you mean, 'What'?" I asked in return as I didn't remember saying anything to her. I'd been gripping the steering wheel in silence for some time. The uphill road was tough going, and I was constantly looking ahead for any oncoming traffic from around the sharp turns. I hadn't the attention to spare to make small talk.

"You were mumbling something," she said.

I realized only then that I had gone from repeating

vaguely remembered snatches of the Heart Sutra in my mind to actually reciting it out loud. Recalling the scene at Mt. Shaka I'd witnessed the previous month automatically made me think of the mantra of the sutra, the part that went *Gaté Gaté*.

"It was nothing," I laughed.

"Weirdo," my wife sighed.

The mantra must have sounded to her like a frog croaking.

I found a wide shoulder on the road and parked the car. The route had been zigzagging uphill for quite some time. The settlement, though, was nowhere to be seen. I'd stopped because I was suddenly worried that we'd ventured onto the wrong road.

Pulling up the handbrake, I turned to the backseat and asked my wife, "Hey, is this really the right way?"

"What? But..." Probably not sure herself, she gave me an anxious look and peered into the map.

Under it I could see the two small faces of my daughters sleeping quietly. I touched their smooth cheeks with my hand. "Let me see it," I said and took the roadmap and faxed directions from my wife's hands.

Trying to figure out if we had taken a wrong turn somewhere, I went back to the starting point on the map and retraced our tracks. I also considered the directions from the old man we'd met along the way. There was no way we'd gotten anything wrong. Assuming the old man had told us the truth, this road was supposed to lead directly to the small settlement of Ura. Still, the thought of there being a settlement this deep in the woods was endlessly puzzling. After the settlement, the road disappeared as if the forest swallowed it up. This was the only route the residents could take to go down the mountain for shopping and other needs, but we'd yet to encounter a single car.

"All right. Let's try going a little further." I gave the map back to my wife.

"I think we're okay…" As if to belie her words, her voice was weaker.

As I faced forward and started to pull out, in the deep V of the valley I could see a single spray of water on the eastern slope. Subterranean creeks gathering across the folds of the mountain were pouring into the Mibu River several hundred yards below. The sun was just setting behind the western ridges, and the boundary between light and shadow was creeping towards the center of the waterfall. Bathed in the last rays of sunlight, the waterfall glittered golden, spilling cool sprays of water down into the river.

"Look, over there. A waterfall," I said, pointing diagonally to the front.

"Where, where?" my wife cried, craning forward and staring at it in awe. As we gazed, the waterfall slipped into the shade, and the golden spray turned silver.

I had experienced the ascetic practice of sitting under a waterfall a month prior. After safely completing the journey from Mt. Shaka to Mt. Yayama and back, I returned to the base lodge in Zenkiguchi. The legless ascetic was waiting for me there as promised. He asked me when I planned to return to Tokyo. When I replied that I was leaving the next day, he invited me to see Uragyoba early the next morning. About three miles from the lodge was a beautiful waterfall called Mie-no-Taki where, he said, Shugendo practitioners trained.

The next morning, I woke up while it was still dark and walked the muddy path with the help of a flashlight. I walked down the dry riverbed and across a mountain stream and climbed up the rocky stretch along the waterfall. The rocks that rose up almost perpendicularly were wrapped in chains, and I had to hoist myself up by grabbing hold of them. I was willing to carry the ascetic on my back if it proved necessary, but he insisted he could climb the rest of the way on his own as long as I lifted him to the tree trunk from halfway up the rock. I did as told, and he crawled up the rocks like a butterfly. The muscles in his arms must have been incredibly well-tempered, having served as his legs on a daily basis.

At the very top of the rocks was the basin of the first of three consecutive waterfalls, the Fudo-daki. In the crisp air, day was just about to break in the eastern sky. The water in the basin shone green with incomparable clarity. I felt an intense urge to soak in that water. The ascetic prompted me to strip down to my underwear. I walked around the basin to the base of the waterfall and folded my legs into the lotus position. For June, there wasn't much water, and the sheet that slipped off the rocks wasn't very thick. Even so, I could feel the intense pressure of the water as it cascaded onto my back. The pressure then morphed into a piercing pain, chilling me to the bone. I couldn't stand it anymore. As I felt the freezing water run in a single stream from my head to my back to my legs, the ascetic gave a cry. Taking that as my cue, I got out of the basin.

My chilled body gradually recovered its heat in June's mild morning weather. At the same time, the sensation of having been refreshed, of the filth and impurities accumulated in my body having been washed away, slowly wrapped around my body.

I was reincarnated. After walking the mountain spurs and getting pounded by the waterfall, I had sloughed off a skin. There I was, exuberant at being alive. There was I, with great expectations for my new job and for watching over my daughters as they grew up.

After the forest of tall cedars came to an end, we caught sight of several old wooden houses on either side of the road. As we realized we'd finally arrived at Ura, my wife and I both sighed in relief.

I figured the log cabin the kids from the kindergarten would stay in had to stand out. Be it on the outskirts of a settlement, the grounds had belonged to an elementary school. It couldn't be hard to find since schools were landmarks of sorts. Still, I slowed down to the lowest possible speed and looked every which way so I wouldn't miss it. I had a preconceived notion that an abandoned school must bear some vestiges of the original buildings. I stopped driving here and there and peered deep into the surrounding settlement. As there were only a few houses dotted along the road, the area wasn't large. From what I could see from the road, however, there didn't seem to be any log cabins that could have been a school.

Before we knew it, the houses had grown sparse, and soon there were none. I thought perhaps the settlement had just ended, but since the directions indicated the cabin was "just outside the settlement," I thought it might show up further beyond. I had no idea how far I was from the center of the settlement, or even where the center was, but there wasn't much distance to travel back. I decided to keep going.

The further we went, the narrower the road got. The gaps between the cedars on each side of the road shrank, creating a tunnel of darkness. Every time the thick, dense shrubs brushed against the sides of the car, they seemed to touch me bodily, making me feel uneasy.

Suddenly the car sank with a thunk, and a troubling vibration welled up from the undercarriage. The paved road had ended, and we were now on a path that was little more than an overgrown animal trail. Feeling as though we'd crossed over into another world, I shivered.

"Hey, let's go back," whined my wife.

Something was strange. There couldn't possibly be an abandoned school beyond here. I wondered if we'd missed it.

"All right. Let's go back," I replied, but there was no space for a U-turn. Some parts along the road were wider, but none sufficiently so. Still, going in reverse back along the road would be a great hassle. Deciding that it would be wiser to look for enough space along the path to make a U-turn, we went on. The center was banked up, and as we drove it felt like the grass sprouting in the middle of the lane was licking the bottom of the car. We couldn't go back even if we wanted to. We were wandering into a dead-end.

Sensing the odd shift in mood, my elder daughter woke up. "Where are we? Are we there? Is Yoko coming, too?" she asked, questioning us as soon as she was awake. When I didn't answer, she nagged, "Hey, hey," redirecting her questions to my wife.

"Just be quiet," my wife refused to answer, staring nervously at the path ahead.

Hearing her sister's voice, my younger daughter awoke,

and the car was suddenly filled with cacophony.

"I'm hungry."

"Can I have a snack?"

"I'm thirsty."

"Where are we?"

"When are we going to get there?"

"Hey, where are we?"

The two vented their frustrations, repeating the same questions. Anxiety rendered their voices more hysterical than usual.

As soon as we turned a broad curve, our field of vision opened up. The cedar forest on the right slope of the valley vanished, turning into a steep rock cliff. It was abruptly bright, as if we'd exited a tunnel. The valley was so steep that the mountain stream flowing along the bottom was nowhere to be seen.

Once they noticed how dizzyingly high we were, both girls cried out at once, "Whoa!" It was unclear whether they'd yelled out of fear or amazement.

The curves became sharper, and as I kept turning the steering wheel to the same direction, the front mask of a minivan appeared just beyond a blind spot. I slammed on the brakes, and our car skidded to a halt, barely avoiding a collision. A license plate marked Matsumoto was right in front of my eyes. The vehicle wasn't coming towards us— it was parked there with the engine still running. I'd never expected to see a van in such a place.

It was parked against the slope of the mountain. Two men stood in the narrow space between the van and the edge as if they meant to peer down the cliff. Both wore khaki work clothes and were face to face, apparently hauling something very heavy along the side of the van. The one closer to us, shocked at the appearance of another car, turned around and let go of the object. Rather than simply drop, it slid from his hips to his knees then from his knees to his feet. What he'd been carrying was the stark naked body of a dead person.

The corpse's bluish black face lolled backwards by the man's feet. At first it looked like a middle-aged woman, but as the man turned around, past his back I could see a penis dangling from the corpse's groin. The other man in work clothes was holding the legs, and the corpse, that of a middle-aged man with a protruding belly, looked as though it was halfway up into a handstand, the back of the head on the ground. From the vacant, half-open eyes to the darkly mottled face and skin, it was clear that he was no longer alive. The situation was self-explanatory. Deep in the mountains, far from civilization, a path that appeared to be a dead-end, a sheer cliff more than several hundred yards high—if one were to toss off a body from there, the chances of anyone finding it were close to zero. If you wanted to dispose of a murder victim, this was much easier than trying to sink the body into the ocean.

A man in a tracksuit appeared from the back of the van. This third man shouted something like an order at the other two, then turned towards us. For a brief moment, our eyes met. He had thinning hair, a rounded face, and a mustache. If I met him on the streets, I'd say he had an affable face. It now wore an expression of total disbelief.

"What on earth…" I was the one who couldn't believe it. What terrible timing. Instead of arriving right after or before, I'd managed to catch them in the middle of the act. Since ancient times, mountains had been regarded as a place where spirits returned after death, and especially lovely peaks were honored as deeply sacred spots. It was not somewhere to dump a corpse, but rather a holy locale for the spirit to sojourn.

Before they could make a move, I shifted into reverse and sped away from the van. The men in work clothes kicked the corpse over the cliff's edge as if they were abandoning unfinished business and scrambled back into the van.

It had all happened in a matter of seconds. My daughters had observed the scene in silence, dumbfounded, but once our car started moving they couldn't stop talking.

"What was that?"

"Daddy, what were those men doing?"

"Daddy, what are you gonna do?"

My daughters demanded a clarification for what they'd just seen, but there was no way to explain it. I didn't know who the men were, why they'd killed that man, or if they were even the ones who'd killed him. I knew nothing.

Those men were throwing a dead body off the cliff.

That was all there was to say. The kids already knew as much. Their young eyes must have discerned that we'd happened upon a terrifying, offensive situation. They were merely unable to understand how that reality related to themselves.

The girls stood up on the backseat and started screaming. Their heads got in the way and I couldn't see the back. If I made one mistake with the handle, we would slide off the edge.

"Shut up!" I shouted to try and get them to sit back down, but they wouldn't listen. All I could do was yell to my wife, "Do something about the kids!"

My wife grabbed them with both arms and fell flat on the seat, curling up and cowering.

"Daddy, Daddy," came thin voices.

The front grill of the van was fast approaching the front of our car. Outrunning them was a lost cause since they were going forward while we were in reverse. They slammed the van repeatedly into the hood of our car, no doubt hoping to toss us witnesses off the cliff too. Irrational violence— terrified, I felt all the blood in my body swiftly drain away. The common term "gut-wrenching" was literally true; past my parched throat the walls of my stomach rapidly contracted, and it was a new type of pain unlike nausea or anything else I had ever experienced.

Through the rearview window, I noticed the road curving to the right. The van thrust its nose into the right shoulder and shoved the side of our car. As I feared, they were trying to push us off. A front wheel came off first, crushed by the fender, and our car skidded forward at an angle, dragging to a stop across the road and blocking the van's progress. Propped up by cedar trees, we'd been saved from hurtling off the precipice.

The two vehicles were at a perpendicular, wedged between the rock face and the cedars, unable to move. Suddenly a loud banging echoed from outside the passenger's side door. One of the men in the van was trying to get out, but with the two cars stuck together, he was having to resort to brute force.

My terrified wife and daughters curled up even tighter.

"Daddy, Daddy," came tearful voices.

I had to banish what was frightening my wife and

daughters, no matter the sacrifice. If this was my fate, I couldn't just sit and watch. *Brace yourself before you shrivel up in fear.* I let the excess tension out of my muscles and imagined losing what I held dear. I couldn't let go of attachments. Even if it meant dirtying my hands, I had to overcome.

I was ready to let *avidya*—ignorance—take over my heart.

I unfastened my seatbelt, lowered the window, and climbed out of the car. I hugged a cedar tree and slid down along the cliff face. *Yield to neither fear nor hatred, lend your body to your natural will to live.*

As I gripped the roots of a shrub and lifted my torso onto the roadside, I noticed that I had a view of the same waterfall I'd spotted earlier. When this was over, how I'd love to be pounded by water to my heart's content. My mind focused on a serene fantasy, what left my lips was a roar—

"Bastards, I'll kill you all!"

Afterword

I tried collecting six works with a common theme—a theme represented by the words "diapers and a race replica." The softness and warmth of diapers, the speed and power of a racer's motorbike—I wished to express a balance of the maternal and the paternal by placing symbols of femininity and masculinity side by side.

In raising children, the maternal and the paternal are both important. If things tip too far one way or the other, they don't go well. I suspect it's a worldwide trend, but in Japan especially, when it comes to childrearing all you hear about is the maternal.

"Only a peaceful and safe world is worth living in"— far too many people seem to think so.

Even when wrongs proliferate, or death approaches, the world is worth it, and I hope to always live by that. I'm not saying you should suck on your thumb and let the world's evils be. If you don't first accept whole the phenomenon that is humanity, which bears evil within itself, you can't take the next step...

While I washed my daughters' cloth diapers, I often entertained such notions. An aspiring novelist married to a schoolteacher, I had no choice but to take on most of our household and childrearing duties. Coming into contact with a newborn's skin, I'd ponder the effect "the paternal" would have on the kids' future. Absent that childrearing experience, this collection would not have been born.

I owe a debt of gratitude to Miruko Yamaguchi at Gentosha. The speed with which she deals with matters never ceases to amaze me. Without the sensible advice, my work would have been nowhere near as tight. You are much appreciated.

Koji Suzuki
September 23, 1995

About the Author

Born in 1957 in Hamamatsu, southwest of Tokyo, Koji Suzuki attended Keio University, where he majored in French. After graduating he held numerous odd jobs including a stint as a tutor. The father of two daughters whom he reared as a struggling writer while his wife worked, he has authored books on childrearing in addition to his blockbuster *Ring* trilogy and other fiction.

Death and the Flower is Suzuki's ninth work to appear in English. He is based in Tokyo but loves to travel, often in the United States.